KT-489-433

PUNITIVE ACTION

Soldiers of Fort Valeau, a Foreign Legion outpost, discover the mutilated bodies of several men from their overdue relief column, ambushed and massacred by Dylaks. Captain Monclaire's radio report to the garrison at Dini Sadazi results in a promise that more soldiers will be despatched to Valeau, from there to mount punitive action against the offenders. But before the reinforcements arrive, the Dylaks send a message to Monclaire — if he does not surrender, they will attack and conquer the fort . . .

Books by John Robb
in the Linford Mystery Library:

JAILBREAK
NO GOLD FOR TINA
FOUR CORPSES IN A MILLION
THE LAST DESERTER
THE BIG HEIST
I SHALL AVENGE!
WE — THE CONDEMNED
ZONE ZERO
MISSION OF MERCY
STORM EVIL
AMERICAN LEGIONNAIRE

JOHN ROBB

PUNITIVE ACTION

Complete and Unabridged

LINFORD
Leicester

First published in Great Britain

First Linford Edition
published 2019

*A catalogue record for this book is available
from the British Library.*

ISBN 978–1–4448–4204–3

Published by
F. A. Thorpe (Publishing)
Anstey, Leicestershire

Set by Words & Graphics Ltd.
Anstey, Leicestershire
Printed and bound in Great Britain by
T. J. International Ltd., Padstow, Cornwall

This book is printed on acid-free paper

An Introduction to Fury...

She was being taken into slavery.

Eager hands pawed at her. Covetous eyes appraised her. But Mademoiselle Maria D'Anton, daughter of a marshal of France, was not afraid.

Yet it seemed that the world was lost to her and only hell remained.

Less than an hour before, she had been travelling with her brother and twelve well-armed guides down the east Morocco coast towards the new trading centre of Mogador. Within two days their long journey from France would have been over. Would have been . . .

They had been telling themselves they were wise to pick the overland caravan route. It was said to be safer, though slower, than the sea.

Now, her brother was dead. So were the guides. And the rich wedding dowry she was taking to her fiancé was being greedily assessed by the barbarous Dylaks. The gold, the silver, her jewellery — even to her small gold locket which contained her father's picture — were all heaped upon the sand.

They told her she was to be taken before El Kavah, Lord of all Morocco in that year of 1860.

And after a week of travel they came to El Kavah's city, remote in the foothills of the Atlas Mountains.

She did not see El Kavah at once. Instead, she was put to live with the serving women. Yet still Maria retained her courage and her strange, arrogant dignity.

It did not desert her when at last she was taken to El Kavah. She had expected to see a man who was fat, sensual, and cruel. She saw none of these things. His features were fine. Finer than those of most Frenchmen, even. And far finer than those of the one she had been due to marry in Mogador. His voice was gentle, his command of the sophisticated French tongue surprisingly perfect. He was young and strong.

He apologised for her treatment.

'I have been absent, mam'selle,' he said. 'Otherwise you would have been freed immediately. You should not have been touched — but I fear that there are many of my people who care little for friendship with the French. I am hoping they will learn. As it is, you are free to go as soon as you wish. And your money, your jewellery — everything will be restored to you.'

He held out the locket.

'I will return this first. I am sure it is of great value to you.'

'It is my father.'

'I know. I am sorry this should have happened to the daughter of Pierre D'Anton.' He smiled at her. It was a mingling of apology and admiration.

She was surprised to find herself smiling, too.

And in that moment Maria D'Anton, raven-haired daughter of a marshal of France, knew that she would never return . . .

3

1

Fort Valeau

Corporal Diepel, the pockmarked Swede, spat out a sodden mess of tobacco. It slapped in front of the file of legionnaires. A fly — a repulsively fat fly — darted over to investigate. Then it flew away, humming its indignation. A rotten corpse, it could enjoy. The more rotten the better. But Corporal Diepel's chewing tobacco — never.

The corporal was preparing to address his section of twelve men. This he did often. He was a great talker, was Diepel. He was also a good soldier.

He said: 'A relief company is due here tomorrow. But you know that, eh? So we start the march for Dini Sadazi as soon as they arrive. You won't be sorry. Nor shall I. This fort is hell. There is no rest here. We'll be well out of it.'

He paused to look at the rejected

tobacco. Then he raised his beady eyes until they rested on the line of motionless men. His face was like an old and mottled nut.

'There was a time,' he continued, 'when service in Fort Valeau meant action. There was fighting. Often there was fighting. The tribes did not like us here. The Dylaks, the Bormones, the Riffs — they tried to finish us. Ah, the Legion meant something in those days!

'But not now! Now, I tell you, we are no more than *gendarmes*. Perhaps there is no need for us. Supposing there is any trouble, what happens? The aeroplanes are sent out. *Boof!* A bomb or two. And the Arabs run. Not that I blame them. I would run, too.'

A sigh, barely audible, came from the centre of the file. It came from Legionnaire Rex Tyle, originally of Brooklyn, New York City, now of *Deux Section*, Company, Second North Moroccan Battalion.

Through motionless lips, Rex whispered: 'That guy will drive me nuts. Mebbe he thinks we like standing here listening to him and sunning ourselves.'

Legionnaire Pete Havers, standing next to him, gave an almost imperceptible nod. His English-accented voice was not so subdued as those of his friend.

'He likes an audience. We are the perfect audience for any orator.'

Corporal Diepel had been mobilising his thoughts for an extension of his diatribe, but the results were never to be made known. For he heard an imperfect fragment of Legionnaire Havers' words. He bristled in the Englishman's direction.

'You! Legionnaire! *Avant* . . . One pace!'

Lebel at the short trail, Pete took a step forward.

There followed a long period of silence, disturbed only by the squawking of a distant carrion bird and the faint moaning of the sand as it shifted constantly under the oven-hot breeze. Diepel looked unblinkingly at Pete. And Pete looked unblinkingly at that part of the compound building which was directly ahead of him.

When Diepel spoke, his words were

pitched in an ominously soft key.

'Perhaps you are not interested in the things I say, Legionnaire?'

Pete turned his head very slightly in the direction of the NCO before attempting a reply. It was a mistake.

'*Attention!* Is it that you think you can walk about on parade like a gigolo in a ballroom? Well . . . is it?'

Pete cleared his throat. There was a pained note in his educated drawl which Diepel (whose knowledge of English was rudimentary) found difficult to follow.

'I don't know, Corporal. I've never studied gigolos. If you would show me how they walk, I'll probably be able to answer.'

From his position in the file, Rex drew in a sharp breath. 'That Limey . . . he's just sitting up and begging for another dose of pack fatigue.'

And he almost winced at the thought. For during his brief twelve months of service, Legionnaire Pete Havers had certainly come near to establishing a record for the number of punishment drills put in for minor disciplinary

8

offences. Which was odd, in a way, because he was a better soldier than most. He took to Legion life with the ease of a man who was no stranger to the military arts. Except for that imperturbable tongue of his. He seemed unable to resist thinly veiled sarcasms towards Corporal Diepel, or even other more senior NCOs. That was a practice which does not pay in any army — least of all in the Legion.

Now Diepel was considering the reply. Slowly, he repeated each word to himself. Then, like an explosion within the brain, the full meaning hit him.

His pitted face contused.

'So! You would be clever, eh? We'll see how clever you are, Legionnaire. Tonight I will speak with Captain Monclaire. I will arrange it so you do no return to Sadazi with the company. Instead, you'll stay here and serve on with the relief garrison. Now what do you think of that, Legionnaire?'

Only a slight narrowing of Pete's eyes revealed any emotion. His voice remained suave, faintly insolent.

'No doubt it is justice. But you'll miss

me, Corporal, and our friendly conversations.'

There was a clatter in the file. A rifle had fallen to the ground. Legionnaire Rex Tyle's rifle. Diepel swung away from Pete. He riveted his malevolent eyes on the Lebel. Then on the American.

'*Batard!* Look at it. You cannot even hold a rifle! You are soft, I say. Soft as women. That, my legionnaire, is an offence under the French Manual of Military Law — as you will soon know. Pick it up!'

Rex's long, lean form bent down and retrieved the weapon. The incident had served its purpose. It had distracted Diepel's attention from the Englishman's last shaft. For now the corporal was expanding on the subject of the modern legionnaire.

' . . . discipline, none. Courage, none. The old legionnaires, the ones who did the fighting, they would weep if they could, but they never knew about tears . . . '

★　★　★

10

The distance from Dini Sadazi to Fort Valeau was three hundred kilometres — or six days' normal marching time. A radio message from Sadazi to the fort had given the relief company's exact time of departure. Therefore their time of arrival could be fixed to within two or three hours. Captain Monclaire, commanding the fort, had fixed it at eight in the evening at the latest.

When eleven o'clock came, and no relief company with it, he began to feel mildly annoyed.

The usual courtesy supper, with the best available wines, had been prepared for the three officers of the incoming company. Monclaire, like all Frenchmen, took his food seriously. Now it would be spoiled. No cook could be expected to keep a main course of *boeuf roti* (even out of cans) in perfect condition for long.

He glanced in exasperation at his watch. Then he looked out of the mess-room window. A full moon was riding high. The fort walls showed clearly, and seemed more impregnable than ever in the thin light. He watched a sentry patrolling the western ramparts. It was from that position that the relief company was due to arrive. And that sentry, from his position forty feet up, would see them when they were still some distance off. Or perhaps he would hear them first. A hundred and twenty men marching on sand and carrying full equipment make a lot of noise.

Having identified the column, it would be the sentry's duty to discharge a single shot. That would bring a sergeant and six men out of the guardhouse to stand by the gates. And the orderly officer would join the sentry on the western rampart.

When the courtesies of recognition were complete, the orderly officer would give the signal, the great gates would swing open, and the six legionnaires and the sergeant would present arms.

Then he, Monclaire, would have supper.

When the relief company arrived.

Monclaire swore gently and turned away from the window.

He looked longingly at the supper table. Laid with white linen, silver condiment sets, thin glasses, ivory-handled cutlery. The last time he'd seen a table looking like that was three months before, when his company had taken over and the previous commanding officer was giving the entertainment.

'*Dieu!*' Monclaire said to himself. 'This is too much. I've always given prompt relief. Why is it that I cannot receive the same courtesy?'

He pulled at his thin moustache, the lean lines of his face clouded with annoyance.

It was strangely typical of Monclaire that he could (and had) faced desperate danger and withering hardship without showing a trace of emotion. Yet the prospect of a spoiled meal created a core of wild resentment in his vitals.

But when midnight came, his reactions began slowly to change.

He left the messroom and walked down a bleak stone corridor to his company office. It was an unnaturally silent place at this hour. And it was in darkness. He lit the two ceiling oil lamps. Then he rang his desk bell.

A bleary-eyed orderly (looking slightly affronted at being called at such an hour) stood to attention before him.

Monclaire finished scribbling a few words on a cypher slip.

They read:

From Commanding Officer Fort Valeau. To Commandant's Secretary, Dini Sadazi. Request repeat of date and hour of departure of relief for this garrison.

He gave the slip to the orderly.

'It is to be despatched immediately,' he said.

When the orderly had gone, Monclaire lit a cigarette and waited.

He was, he knew, running a strong risk of looking extremely foolish. Any number of trivialities could have accounted for the lateness of the relief company's arrival. But the point was that they never *were* late. The march, though long, had for years been covered with almost mathematical precision. So it was necessary to be sure that there had been no error in the advised time of departure.

Twenty minutes later the reply came crackling over the three hundred kilometres of barren sand. In another two minutes the Morse was transcribed and on Monclaire's desk.

. . . Company departed 16 hours, July 17.

There had been no mistake.

Monclaire hesitated, put on his cap, strode out of the office and on to the open square. He hunched his shoulders slightly against the cold bite of the Moroccan night. A light showed through the guardroom window. He moved towards it.

The sentry clicked to attention, brought his Lebel to the slope, and slapped the butt in salute. Monclaire acknowledged with a wave of his cane as he entered the guardroom.

There was an atmosphere of confined humanity in there. Three men were dozing on wall bunks. Three others and the sergeant were standing in a short, stiff file while Lieutenant Gina, the orderly officer, went through the formality of examining the report book. Gina was a young, pallid, conscientious officer. He looked almost annoyed at the interruption as he saluted Monclaire.

Monclaire asked: 'No sign of the relief yet?'

'*Non, mon capitaine*. Do you . . . do you think anything could have gone wrong?'

'Certainly not.'

He was annoyed as he left the guardroom.

The lieutenant, Monclaire told himself, should have shown more intelligence and restraint. To ask a question of that nature in front of several legionnaires showed the depths of stupidity. Within a few hours the whole fort would be seething with a rumour that something had happened to the relief company. The fact that he had firmly denied the possibility of anything happening to them would not count for much. His words would be either ignored or distorted.

He decided to take an early opportunity for a crisp private interview with

Lieutenant Gina. The fellow meant well
. . . but he was still in swaddling clothes
so far as military experience went. And he
must learn that officers did not discuss
administrative questions in front of the
men.

Monclaire mounted the thirty-four
stone steps let into the west wall. These
took him onto the ramparts. The sentry
was some yards distant, and moving away.
There was a sense of lofty isolation up
here. He found it soothing, satisfying.

The moon touched the sand with
silver. It looked almost like the sea. And
the dunes, rolling into infinity, could be
the waves. He felt like a lonely god
looking upon a deserted kingdom.

But it was not the time for reverie. With
an effort, he tried to make an appreciation of his position.

Obviously, *something* had delayed the
relief. But what? Men falling ill, or
accidental injury? No. There was a
medical unit with each company, and the
sick could be carried on stretchers slung
between the pack mules.

A sandstorm? That was a possibility,

but improbable. Such storms were seldom localised. They swept over hundreds or thousands of square miles. And there had been no suggestion of one here . . .

Monclaire lit yet another cigarette and tossed the glowing match over the wall.

Years ago — it seemed many years ago — he would have feared that the company had been attacked. But this, so far as Morocco was concerned, was the age of peace. Why, not one in ten of his men had seen a shot fired in anger. And those who had were nearly all long-service NCOs; like the verbose Corporal Diepel, for example, who had come to him that evening with yet another complaint about that Englishman, Legionnaire Havers . . .

Suddenly there was a shaft of amber in the sky. Monclaire turned. The abrupt African dawn was breaking. He glanced at his watch. It was four o'clock.

Below, in the fort square, there was a shuffle of movement then the bark of commands. The guard was being changed.

And the chill was fading out of the air.

The first hint of the day's heat was caressing his skin. It was pleasant for the moment. Soon it would be an oven-like hell.

He was moving towards the steps when he heard the sentry shout.

'*Mon capitaine!* Look!'

The sentry was leaning against a rampart and pointing across the sand.

There was something there — something perhaps three hundred yards away. But the light was not yet strong enough for him to make out what it was. It looked like a heaving, writhing, shadowy heap. As he ran down the steps, Monclaire thought: 'It could be a dying camel. It's about the right size.'

But some instinct told him that it was not a camel.

At the bottom he gave a couple of sharp orders.

'Lieutenant Gina, call out the reserve guard. Sergeant, you and three men come with me.'

The great double gates were unbarred and pushed open by grunting legionnaires.

Monclaire led the way at a half-run across the tugging sand and sharp rock.

They were still several yards from the spot when they stopped. They had to stop. It was the compulsion of horror.

No camel was there.

Just seven legionnaires and an officer.

They lay lashed together with hemp thongs, while the warming sand drank greedily of their spilling blood. Two or three were already dead. The others whimpered and twisted in the final contortions. For knives had been used to do demonic things to them.

The medical orderlies came out with stretchers. With the strange tenderness that men can show to other men, they were carried into the fort and thence to the sick bay.

There the medical officer was waiting, a white coat over his uniform, instruments already sterilising in a tray beside the operating table.

The medical officer was a man of long experience. He had served in the Riff rebellion, the operations against El Dowla, and recently in Indo-China. He had seen thousands die in every possible variety of circumstances. But he let go a hiss of unrestrained emotion when the stretchers were laid before him.

Then he pointed briefly to three figures. They were taken to the mortuary.

Captain Monclaire watched while the doctor made a quick examination of the others.

And when it was done, he asked: 'Have they any chance?'

The MO was holding a hypodermic syringe to the light. He shook his head.

'I can make the end easier for them — that is all . . . '

A legionnaire who had been coughing and muttering suddenly forced himself to a half-sitting posture, a hand clutching the slashed mess that had been his stomach. He gazed around him like a child awakening from a nightmare. Monclaire crossed to him and put a hand on his blood-soaked tunic.

'*Mon ami*, are you from the relief company?'

At first it seemed that he did not comprehend. Then he fixed his dull, flat eyes on Monclaire. He gave the faintest hint of a nod.

'Tell me . . . what happened?'

He was a German. The guttural words came hollowly.

'*Bitte* . . . leave me . . . '

He moaned, still holding his belly. Then, without warning, he slumped forward off the stretcher and onto the stone floor.

As the orderlies took him away, Monclaire looked almost desperately at the other dying men. Then he turned to the medical officer, who had finished adjusting the syringe.

'Listen! Never mind about relieving their pain . . . not until you have fixed one of them so he can speak. I *must* know what happened . . . *must* . . . the officer . . . he still lives . . . can you make him conscious for just a minute?'

The medical officer took up another syringe. He looked at it doubtfully.

'I could inject adrenalin. It might work. But, *Dieu*! It would be cruel . . . cruel.'

Monclaire compressed his lips. Then, scarcely opening them, he breathed: 'I know that. But . . . the relief company has been attacked! It is incredible, but it must be so. And if one of them does not talk, we'll never know who did it, or when, or how. The officer can best tell me . . . if you can get him to talk!'

The medical officer shrugged his shoulders. He kneeled beside a stretcher where a young, dark-haired man lay, breathing heavily and irregularly, his uniform in tatters but his captain's badges of rank still incongruously undamaged.

The needle went into the unconscious officer's arm. The plunger was pressed down.

Then Monclaire, too, kneeled at the stretcher, watching the slack, immobile face. It was vaguely familiar. All of a sudden, he placed it. He had last seen this officer when on staff duty at Algiers. Paul Rene had been a junior lieutenant then, not long out of St. Cyr. A brilliant future had been forecast for him — and with good reason, for he had an excellent military brain. He must have come with recent replacements to Sadazi.

Monclaire thought: 'He was doing better than me. He gained his captaincy much sooner than I did. He would have been a great soldier of France . . . '

He was dimly surprised to find himself already thinking of the man in the past tense. That was wrong. Captain Rene was not gone yet. And he must not go until he had spoken . . .

Involuntarily, he grasped Rene's shoulder and tried to shake it. The medical officer pulled the arm away.

'That will not help, *capitaine*.'

Monclaire cursed and mumbled an apology.

A minute passed. A minute of leaden hell. Rene's noisy breathing continued. But his eyes stayed closed.

Monclaire looked towards where the medical officer was injecting morphia into the others.

'He's not going to recover. Can't you try some more of the drug?'

'An overdose would kill him immediately. You must be patient.'

It was then that Captain Rene muttered an incomprehensible word. It could have been anything, but it was an attempt at articulation.

This time, but with difficulty, Monclaire restrained a desire to touch him.

Slowly, like those of a doll, Rene's eyes opened. And at the same moment his mouth tightened and twisted in a reaction to pain.

Monclaire gathered himself. This was his one flickering chance. If it slipped away, there would be no other. Lips close to Rene's ear, he said: 'I am Monclaire, commanding Fort Valeau. Tell me . . . '

Rene interrupted with a cough. The medical office came over to wipe blood from his lips.

Monclaire started again: 'I am . . . '

He stopped because Rene's eyes were upon them. They looked startlingly young and blue and unwavering. Then his right hand, filthy and contused from the bonds, wavered towards his breast. It groped feebly at the breast-pocket button. Gradually, the groping became less, until only one finger twitched. Then that stopped too.

But those eyes were still upon Monclaire. As though he had wanted to speak.

The medical officer pulled down the lids.

'I'm sorry, *capitaine*. I feared it would be no use.'

But Monclaire was not listening. He was looking at Rene's breast pocket. It bulged slightly.

He removed the lifeless fingers from the security button. He unfastened the flap and drew out a roll of buff paper.

He recognised it at once without reading the printed heading, or the scrawled words beneath.

It was the official form on which officers had to describe immediately any incident, large or small, in which their troops had been engaged.

It was known as an After-Action Report.

Monclaire offered a silent prayer of thanks.

Then, clutching the paper in a sweating hand, he strode towards his office.

In parts, Rene's report was almost indecipherable. That was easy to understand. It had been written in the last ghastly moments before capture. And, by some quirk of fate, the Dylaks had not found it or bothered about it.

The relief company had been attacked

while bivouacked for the night, and while only a single day's march from the fort. Because it was unexpected, it was devastating. At first, Dylak tribesmen on foot had broken into the northern perimeter, and fired the tents with burning brands.

Then cavalry had followed. Several hundred well-trained horsemen had forced the company into the centre of the burning inferno and opened on them with light automatic weapons ... the report was quite clear about that — automatic weapons. It was astonishing, but an officer of Rene's calibre would not make a mistake about such a matter, even under such circumstances.

The final words were: ' . . . *less than a dozen of us left. I have . . .* '

And there it broke off.

Monclaire dropped the report on his desk and sunk his head into his hands. It was not difficult to imagine the rest.

Rene and the seven others had been unfortunate enough to be captured alive. So they had become objects of amusement to the Dylaks. Objects of repulsive surgery upon the belly which reduced the toughest and the bravest of men to gibbering insanity within a few minutes.

Then they had been deposited outside the fort during the previous night. No doubt intended as a warning of some sort.

Monclaire gazed remotely at the opposite wall.

He asked himself hollowly: '*Nom de Dieu!* But why . . . why?'

He could conceive of no answer.

Major tribal trouble had become unknown. Occasionally (but only very occasionally) there had been minor skirmishes with renegade Bormones who had tried to raid Arab caravan routes. But that was all.

But the Dylaks — and Rene had been specific in naming them — had long since withdrawn to the eastern foothills of the Atlas Mountains, where the French had been glad to leave them to their own apparently peaceful devices.

Yet there was no denying that a baffling and critical situation had arisen in which an entire company had been massacred.

28

Wearily, Monclaire drew a cypher pad towards him and prepared to send a radio signal to Dini Sadazi.

2

Mobilisation

Colonel Jean Panton, commanding the garrison at Dini Sadazi, adjusted his spectacles on a fat nose. He re-read Monclaire's signal with the incredulous astonishment of a child at a conjuring performance. But he was not entirely displeased. At the back of his mind an idea was taking shape . . .

The colonel had not attained his rank through being a fool, neither had he reached it through virtue of an outstanding ability. He was a mediocrity. But essentially a crafty mediocrity.

From the day he emerged from St. Cyr military academy, he had followed what he conceived to be a sound professional principle. In short, it was to lose no opportunity of humiliating his subordinates, and never to fail to fawn upon his superiors.

30

As a result, those above him regarded Colonel Panton as a sound soldier — for he never disputed their decisions. Those below regarded him in another light — for he almost always overruled them.

Most officers would have been content to regard the Sadazi command as a satisfactory climax to a career. But not Colonel Panton.

The colonel sought yet higher things. The High Command at Algiers, perhaps . . . or even the General Staff in Paris . . .

But he was shrewd enough to know that before such things became possible he must first produce some indisputable proof of ability.

Some decisive military stroke was needed. A stroke bearing the genius of a Ney, or a Foch, or — yes — even Napoleon.

Yet there had been no such opportunity — until now.

Now, it seemed, the supreme moment was at hand.

He read the signal yet again, though he knew it by heart.

His first course was obvious. He would have to communicate with the Deputy Chief of the High Command. Then, in due course, the High Command would make recommendations for punitive action, and arrangements for any necessary reinforcements.

But suppose — and Colonel Panton licked his fleshy lips at the prospect — suppose he were to act immediately on his own initiative? And present the command with a *fait accompli*?

If he were to do that, the future would be rich with success.

It happened that the colonel was a secret actor. He was one of those men who, when unobserved, like to act imaginary scenes in which they themselves play a vital and heroic part.

He was inspired to enact one now.

He stood up and peeped through the window. Save for the sentries at the gates, the parade ground was deserted.

Then to the door. The orderlies were busy at their typewriters in the outer room.

Quietly, he slipped home the bolt.

He smoothed his tunic over a pear-shaped belly. Carefully, he put on his glittering silver-braided cap. Then, advancing smartly on his own desk, he gave a quivering salute.

'*Mon general*,' he said firmly, 'I have to formally report that the Dylaks have been traced and destroyed. Their insurrection could have caused widespread unrest, so I deemed it necessary to strike immediately . . . And I directed the operation personally!'

He paused, listening to inaudible words of praise from a non-existent general. He even contrived a faint blush of affronted modesty.

Then: 'The general is too kind . . . a recommendation to the staff . . . it is a great reward for a humble soldier who only tried to do his duty . . . '

He saluted again at the empty chair, turned smartly about and unbolted the door.

Still in the beatific haze of his daydream, Colonel Panton pressed a bell and prepared to direct a large-scale punitive action against the Dylaks.

The graves were already filled. They were those of Captain Rene and his seven legionnaires. They were buried in the small consecrated spot just outside the fort's north wall.

Quietly, Monclaire had read the prescribed service. He had watched the hurriedly constructed coffins, each covered with a Tricolour, lowered into the depths. Heard the crash of saluting musketry from the guard of honour.

Then, back in his office, Colonel Panton's message awaited him.

'It's just come through,' Lieutenant Gina said, his normally pallid face flushed with excitement. And he waited anxiously while Monclaire read the cypher slip.

From: Commandant, Dini Sadazi. To: Commanding Officer, Fort Valeau. Am leaving at 12.00 hours this day with three companies plus half a battery of horse artillery. Destination Fort Valeau. Fort will be used as base for punitive expedition against Dylaks.

Monclaire made no comment as he inserted the slip in his desk file.

Lieutenant Gina decided to risk a comment.

'It looks as though the colonel means business.'

Monclaire lit a cigarette; then, remembering, offered one to Gina. He inhaled deeply before answering.

'The colonel,' he said, 'is a damned fool.'

Gina looked shocked and pained. He was young enough to regard any colonel commandant as an automatic object of veneration. And he had never heard Monclaire speak of a senior officer in such terms before. But then it was Gina's good fortune that he had seldom come into contact with Panton. Monclaire had.

'I don't understand. It seems like strong action to me. And surely that's what is needed. If the Dylaks are not punished quickly, the whole of Morocco could be aflame. Like it was ten years ago when . . .'

He caught Monclaire's eyes and trailed off, surprised at his own temerity.

It was not that Monclaire looked hostile. Merely that he seemed both pained and amused. But his tones were quite kindly.

'Tell me,' he said, 'what is the garrison establishment of this fort?'

'Why — er — one hundred and twenty-three.'

'Precisely. One hundred and twenty-three, not including four officers and sixteen NCOs. Now, would you say we have room to spare?'

Gina removed both his cap and the sweat from his brow which was not entirely due to the heat.

'Of course . . . we will be overcrowded.'

'Overcrowded! *Mon ami*, it will be an inferno. This is a small fort. It can neither accommodate nor feed the four hundred extra men that Panton is bringing without gross confusion. Yet his plan might be tolerable if it showed any tactical virtue. But it does not. In my opinion, it is merely stupid. And I have no doubt they tried to tell him so in Sadazi — but the colonel never listens.'

Gina was genuinely curious.

'Stupid — why?'

'Because it is highly unlikely the Dylaks will strike in this area again. *If* they strike again. They are far more likely to lie in wait for other relief columns going out to other forts.'

'If that is so, what is the answer?'

'To do what should have been done years ago — equip each column with wireless. Then they can immediately report an attack. And have mobile columns in selected areas so that they can come to their aid. I can see no other answer.'

'Air bombing?'

'*Non*. That is only useful when the enemy can be positively identified from the air. It has been used with good effect on rebel bases, but at the moment we don't know exactly where our enemy is. Pilots may attack a big concentration of Arabs, only to learn later that they are — or were — friendly.'

Monclaire rose from where he had been sitting at the corner of his desk and looked at his watch.

'The colonel will be leaving within an

hour. Send a formal acknowledgement to him. We'll do all we can to make him comfortable, but I'm glad to say that it won't be much.'

★ ★ ★

Legionnaire Rex Tyle, on duty on the west ramparts, swore mildly. Then, dissatisfied with his first effort, he swore again with greater vigour.

He had just started the second hour of his four-hour stretch. It was shortly after midday and the sun was at the shrivelling zenith of intensity. It penetrated his *kapak* and attacked the nape of his neck. It penetrated his tunic and set his body sweat boiling. It reflected from the desert sand and started his eyes aching.

But that was not all. There was also the dismal thought that if all men had justice, he and the rest of the garrison (with the possible exception of Pete Havers) would now be on their way back to Sadazi.

At first, like the others, Rex had forgotten his disappointment under the excitement of the news of the Dylak attack. But now that a few hours had passed, now that he was alone, he had time to consider his misfortune.

He admitted to himself that there was not a lot to attract a man in Sadazi. It was a stinking, fly-bitten garrison town. The only entertainment worthwhile came out of a bottle in the wine shops.

It was not to be compared with Times Square, with a quick slug of Bourbon in Jack Dempsey's bar on the corner of 47th Street, with a look-see at a leg show on Broadway . . .

But he guessed that all life was a matter of comparison. And by comparison with Fort Valeau, Sadazi was paradise.

He thought about the fort and cursed yet again. He thought about Sadazi. Then his mind returned to New York City. To Brooklyn in particular.

It seemed like another age, that night when he returned to his lodging room after a day's work in an automobile garage. And he sat on the sagging bed and counted out the money from his pay envelope. Forty-two dollars and eleven cents. That was one week's wages in advance, paid out to him after he had socked the garage foreman across the jaw.

Sitting on that bed, he had got round to thinking. The foreman hadn't been such a bad guy. Maybe the foreman had been right to keep picking on him. Maybe his work wasn't so good.

Then why had he fallen for that sudden impulse to hit him?

Nerves, he guessed. He had always been jumpy, unsettled, and resentful ever since he was given an honourable discharge from the United States Army at the end of the war.

He'd been okay while he was a GI. Served with the 117th Infantry Regiment in Italy. Then to England to train for that bloody landing on Juno Beach on 6th June 1944. Fought right across Normandy and France to the Rhine. It was at the Rhine that he was wounded and got himself a Purple Heart.

So, still sitting motionless on that bed, he'd figured it out that he was a no-good guy as a civilian. The army was the only life he knew. The only life he understood. The army and action.

Action . . . That put Uncle Sam's outfit right out of the picture. Maybe he'd be better in uniform again — but not stamping around on a parade ground all the time.

It was then that he had thought of the Legion. He'd read newspaper articles about it by guys who'd served and come out. When he was a kid, he'd read the novels of Wren . . .

Maybe he'd fit in there.

So he'd worked his passage in a freighter to Marseilles. There he had enlisted for five years at the Legion recruiting headquarters.

That was two years ago.

And what had he done since then, in his time as a legionnaire?

Rex eased the sling of his Lebel where it was biting against his shoulder. And he clicked his dry tongue.

He'd done six months' training in Marseilles. Cursed and blasted at in a way that would have caused a mutiny in any GI outfit. But he hadn't minded that so much, because he'd thought maybe he'd see some action when it was over.

Action!

He snorted.

Nine months in Algiers doing patrols in the native quarters, with an occasional insult from an Arab as the nearest thing to excitement.

Then to Dini Sadazi, where a punk of a colonel thought it smart to have every man not on desert patrol doing five hours' arms drill a day. Even those desert patrols produced nothing more interesting than balloon-sized blisters on the big toe.

After that, three months in this goddam fort.

And now, the day they were due to be relieved, the other garrison had gone and got itself cut up in the first bit of action the Legion had seen in years. It wouldn't be so bad if it meant that he was going to see something happen too. But he didn't kid himself. Those Arabs'd keep well away from this area now. There'd be no fighting while Legionnaire Rex Tyle was around.

'I guess I'm a one-man peace treaty,' he told himself darkly. 'They oughta have me on the staff of the United Nations . . . '

And, standing there on the ramparts, he brooded on.

Rex did not know it, but he was the natural product of the age. The age which had taken boys as its raw material, and tempered them to manhood in the cauldron of a world war.

He had been moulded in an atmosphere of courage, fear, and to-hell-with-everything. Like many others, he could not shake it off. It had become part of him. A bequest of a crazy century . . .

Slowly, the sweat-filled minutes passed, and clotted stickily into another hour.

By this time, Rex was beyond the luxury of retrospective contemplation. His mind had become centred entirely on one immediate prospect. The prospect of getting off the ramparts, stripping out of his wet uniform, and flopping down on his bunk.

Less than an hour — then he'd be able to do just that. He paced slowly, the heat from the stone striking up through his boots and burning the soles of his feet.

At the angle of the ramparts he met Legionnaire Anoti, who was on duty on the north wall. Anoti, an Italian, had the aspect of a man who had been broiled alive and did not care. They nodded to each other and turned their backs. Talking was forbidden. In any case, neither of them felt like even a brief whispered exchange.

Rex heard Anoti's retreating steps echoing his own.

Crush-slunch, crush-slunch, crush-slunch.

It annoyed him, that noise. He wanted to turn and shout to the little Italian: 'Hell, can't you stop that row with your boots!'

Then he stopped and told himself: 'Nerves again. Nerves and the heat. You gotta take a hold of yourself.'

He turned and gazed over the ramparts at the shimmering waste of undulating sand.

All there exactly as usual. As it had been from the beginning of time, and would be to the end. Just sand. Patches of fine sand that worked into the boots, over the body, into the eyes and the hair and made a guy feel like he was being rubbed over with abrasive paper. Patches of rock. Sharp-edged rock that could cut like a razor. Small, round rock on which a man could break an ankle.

All there. All exactly as usual.

But it wasn't.

Hell, it wasn't!

In the middle distance, robes flapping, was a long line of Arab horsemen.

3

The Gates

There were standing orders for most eventualities in Fort Valeau. One of them came under the title of 'The Approach of a Person or Persons from the Desert Area'.

And it stated that in such an eventuality the sentry making the observation must immediately do one of two things. He must call an NCO if one was within hailing distance. Otherwise, he must fire a single shot vertically.

The nearest NCO — which chanced to be Corporal Diepel — was in the guardroom. And the guardroom, far below and just inside the gates, was easily within the range of a well-pitched voice.

So Rex shouted, according to orders: 'Observation!'

For a moment nothing happened. Then Corporal Diepel emerged, ramming his cap on a glistening bald head. He turned his pitted face up and bawled: 'What is it, Legionnaire?'

'Arabs. Mounted Arabs. Armed. And there's one helluva lot of them.'

Diepel showed no emotion. With almost ridiculous slowness he mounted the thirty-four steps to the west ramparts. He had the guardroom field glasses slung round his neck. With the same precise deliberation he extracted them from their battered leather case. He looked through them for a long time while Rex glanced alternately at him and at the horsemen.

Then Diepel lowered the glasses and turned an expressionless face towards where a runner waited outside the guardroom.

'Legionnaire! Message to the orderly officer. The orderly corporal requests his presence on the west wall.' In spite of Diepel's flat tones, the runner seemed to sense urgency. Ignoring the blistering heat, made worse by the confinement of the fort walls, he departed for the duty office at a fast run.

Meantime, Diepel cut himself a chunk

of black tobacco and started to chew.

Rex had been about to ask him what he'd seen through the glasses — thereby risking a disciplinary tirade, or worse. But the question could not be asked while Diepel was dealing with a new plug of tobacco. At the moment, his jaws were working to reduce the stuff to that sort of soft consistency which would not impede his free speech when the orderly officer arrived.

The orderly officer was Lieutenant Gina. The runner intercepted him as he was about to leave Monclaire's office.

Before the message was complete, Monclaire picked up his field glasses from the desk and moved quickly out of the room.

On the ramparts Diepel pushed his tobacco into the corner of his mouth, saluted, and said: 'Over there, *capitaine*.'

Monclaire raised his field glasses. Gina stared over his shoulder. And Rex stared from a more respectful distance.

One fact was becoming obvious to all of them; it was that the Arabs had no immediate interest in the fort. They were riding fast, and the leaders were turning in a slightly easterly direction.

Gina said: 'They'll be out of sight in a few minutes.'

Monclaire did not answer at first. Then, still peering through his glasses, he answered: 'I think not. They are going to pitch camp.'

Involuntarily, Gina said: '*Dieu*, but why?'

'Those men are Dylaks . . . now can you imagine why?'

There was no answer. So Monclaire added: 'They probably are doing no more than presenting us with a show of strength. An attempt at intimidation, if you wish. They will be feeling most confident now that they have massacred a Legion company.'

'Then — then does this mean that the whole of the Dylak people are in revolt?'

'*Oui*.'

'But it is madness! With the resources at the command of France, they could only achieve their own destruction.'

'Perhaps, but such an argument has never deterred any people who are bent on war.' Monclaire lowered his glasses and went on slowly: 'And I have a feeling that there is more — much more — in all this than a simple tribal revolt. There is something . . . a little ominous about it all. Take the attack on the relief garrison. It was obviously executed skilfully. And Rene's after-action report referred to automatic weapons. And it came without any warning at all. There was never a hint of trouble from the Dylaks. It all suggests to me the most careful planning and preparation which may have been going on for years. And if that is so, there will be a purpose behind it, *mon ami*. A purpose which is far more profound than merely making a few nuisance attacks on Legion columns — or even Legion forts.'

It was then that Monclaire was proved correct on one point — the long line of horsemen had halted and already a scattering of skin tents was appearing.

But that was not all.

As Monclaire looked again through the glasses, he said: '*Dieu!* We are about to have visitors.'

Three Dylaks were riding towards the

fort. One of them was holding his long sabre aloft. A square of white material was fluttering from it.

The gates were opened for them and the three horsemen rode into the fort.

Immediately, they were covered by the rifles of the duty guard. But, unheeding, they rode into the centre of the compound. There, Gina — a slightly nervous Gina — awaited them.

One of the Dylaks raised his sabre in salute. Gina was uncertain about the correctness of it, but he returned the courtesy. Then this Dylak said, in tolerable French: 'We wish to speak with the officer commanding. Are you he?'

Gina shook his head. He was uncomfortably aware that almost all the garrison who were on duty, and a great many of those who were not, were listening to every word and studying his reactions.

'*Non*. I am the orderly officer of the day. But wait, and I will enquire whether Captain Monclaire will see you.'

As he turned towards the administrative block, Gina decided that he had acquitted himself satisfactorily. It was a nice touch to keep them waiting while he made a quite unnecessary enquiry.

Monclaire was at his desk. He looked surprised when Gina entered.

'Well . . . ?'

'It's as you thought. They wish to speak with you.'

'Then why aren't they here?'

'I — I thought it better not to make it seem too easy.'

Monclaire's lean face clouded. For a second it looked as though he was going to make an acid comment. But instead, he said quietly: 'Escort them in.'

And as Gina strutted importantly out, Monclaire wondered briefly whether he ought to have told him that Dylak Arabs regarded it as an affront if they were kept waiting — and there was no point in insulting them at this stage. But, he decided, it was purely due to inexperience. And he wondered whether the massacre of the relief column was to some degree due to inexperience, too. It was so long since the Legion had been in action in Morocco. So many of the men were green. If it came to the test, would they have the unbreakable toughness of those old campaigners, most of whom had long since been discharged?

Somehow, Monclaire doubted it. No doubt, they would learn in time. But time might not be granted to them. It was not granted to the legionnaires of the relief company.

The three Dylaks came into the small room. They were tall men. They seemed to fill and dominate the place.

Monclaire appraised them swiftly. Their grey-white robes were well brocaded, but not richly so. But they were, he noticed, exceptionally voluminous. Idly, he wondered why.

Their appearance was typical. Strong noses; narrow, almost slanting eyes; jutting and sparsely bearded chins. Each of them was in his prime of physical strength.

But it was not their apparel or looks which interested Monclaire most. It was something far more unusual.

It was the Piet automatic rifles which were slung across the back of their shoulders.

They were modern and viciously effective weapons; only issued to a few Western armies, and *then* solely for the use of special service units. Certainly the Legion had never used them. They stuck to their forty-year-old Lebels.

So those were the automatic weapons to which Rene had referred in his hurriedly scrawled after-action report . . .

The middle Dylak took a pace forward so that he was within inches of the desk.

He did not waste time. He said: 'You are able to speak with the Commandant at Dini Sadazi?'

Monclaire hesitated and nodded.

'*Oui*. We are in wireless communication.'

The Dylak smiled. It was thin and humourless.

'Then you must take some advice, *capitaine*. Use your wireless. Tell them at Dini Sadazi that if you do not surrender this fortress to us now, it will fall to us before the sun is down.'

Monclaire had been leaning back in his chair. Involuntarily, he jerked upright. As the full impact of the words drove home he regarded the Dylak with a blend of anger and astonishment.

Then he said icily: 'Repeat that.'

It was repeated word for word. Even the vocal intonations were exactly reproduced.

'Who — who ordered you to bring this — this ludicrous message?'

'That matters not, *capitaine*. It came from one who knows.'

There was a deathly certainty about the way he spoke. Indifference, too. Like a man discussing an event which was due to take place a hundred years hence.

Monclaire was confused. He did not show it, but he admitted it to himself. The Dylaks, he remembered, had certain usual characteristics. Courage, cruelty, and duplicity. Those were they. But exaggeration, *non*. That was not their habit.

Yet . . . to speak of the fort falling before sundown was the essence of nonsense. It could hold out indefinitely against attack from the Dylak cavalry outside. Machine guns would decimate them before they got near the walls. Their automatic rifles, decisive in open battle, would be useless against a fort.

Monclaire leaned forward. He sought the eye of the Dylak warrior, who met his gaze with that same unwavering indifference.

Speaking slowly, Monclaire said: 'I do not know what madness causes you to bring a message of this kind. I do not much care. But note my words carefully and take them back . . .

'Your people received no interference from France since they went back to their hills below the mountains. France was glad to leave you in peace. But now — but a few hours ago you made a treacherous attack upon a Legion column. You struck in the night, when your enemy slept, like carrion birds at their prey . . .

'Then you defiled and tortured a few of the survivors and left them dying outside these walls . . . '

Monclaire rose slowly to his feet. Under the deep tan, his face was grey with anger. His eyes, as they held those of the Dylak, glittered with fury.

'These are crimes for which France will make you pay. For them, you and your people will suffer as few have suffered before. You may run, but we will hunt you. And in the end we will find you. Then you will receive the same mercy that you showed those legionnaires who died in the night . . .

'Now go, and take my words with you . . . '

As his voice ceased there was a sudden silence in the hot, little room. A silence that seemed to bear down and threaten to crush.

It was broken when the foremost Dylak shrugged and rustled his robes. Then the three turned and swept out, Gina following.

Monclaire pulled a handkerchief from his tunic sleeve. He was sweating even more than the heat warranted. His heart was crashing against his ribs. And his mind was in a tumult of confusion and fury.

Never, never in all his years of service had he heard of a situation like this! Dylak cavalry informing a Legion officer that he had better surrender his fort! A fort which had not even been attacked. It was intolerable!

Breathing heavily, he rose and gazed out of the window.

The Dylaks were there, mounting their horses while Gina stood by. The gates were being reopened and a dozen legionnaires were standing by them with unslung rifles.

The Dylaks had touched spurs to their horses and now they were cantering gently towards the gates.

Again Monclaire noticed those robes they were wearing. Not only did they seem larger than usual, but they looked as though they were secured in some special way, for they did not billow out as the breeze caught them . . .

The next few seconds were a flash from the depths of hell.

In the first of them (the ominous prelude) the Dylaks were almost level with the gates, riding line abreast.

In the next they had produced long, thin sticks of yellow-brown material.

In the third second they had hurled the

sticks at the open gates.

There followed one infinitesimal fraction when time was held in vacuum.

Then a purple streak of flame leapt across the gates and upwards inside the west wall. The earth itself seemed to explode from within. Eardrums contracted then expanded under the pressure of the blast and the thunder of exploding gelignite.

And the west side of the fort disappeared in a thick swirling cloud of sand through which could be heard the regular thud of falling debris.

The cloud cleared.

And where the three Dylaks and their horses had been there was now nothing, save a ghastly mess of churned and charred flesh, the blood of the beasts mingling with the blood of men.

Where the legionnaires had been there was nothing, save the same shapeless, awful remnants.

And the gates of Valeau were no more.

4

Battle of the Breach

Monclaire saw it from the garrison office window. The glass shattered in on him, inflicting jagged cuts on his face, but he was not aware of it.

Rex saw it from the west ramparts. He had been about to be relieved and he was waiting, with rifle at the slope, at the centre of the wall. This was some distance from the gates. But even so, he was nearly thrown off the narrow ledge and on to the ground forty feet below.

Lieutenant Gina saw it from where he was standing in the compound. He was thrown on his back and his left arm was fractured by a flying fragment of wood.

Corporal Diepel saw it from the door of the guard-room. The blast blew him inside the stone building, and that saved his life, although it nearly fractured his skull.

And Legionnaire Pete Havers saw it from the barred windows of the detention cell, where he was spending his off-duty hours in penance for insubordination to an NCO. A very English understatement escaped from Pete as he picked himself up off the floor.

'This,' he said, 'is a distinctly poor show.'

But his dry, cultured accent was blended with a mighty roar which swept to the fort from across the sand.

The Dylaks were charging.

Monclaire had his moments of hesitation. Moments when a reeling mind refused to grasp and could not react to the calamity. It was instinct that took him out of his glass-spattered office. It was instinct that made him pick up his pistol belt on the way and hook it to his waist.

But even as he stood in the compound he still had no clear idea of what to do.

The gates are gone . . . the gates are gone . . . gone . . . gone . . .

The words hammered in his head slowly, deliberately, like the tolling of a funeral bell.

It was the sight of Lieutenant Gina which cleared his mind. Gina was standing opposite him. His left arm was hanging twisted, like a length of soft wire. His features were twisted, too. But with his sound arm he saluted. A very formal salute. And he said: 'A barricade, *mon capitaine*?'

Monclaire looked at him as though he were a dream which had become indisputable reality. This was Gina! This was the crude, fumbling subaltern! The officer who had never been in action before! Yet here was Gina, wracked with pain, pointing out exactly what must be done!

For he was right. Obviously right. Somehow, in some way, that yawning gap where the gates had been must be filled. Filled immediately.

Monclaire ran towards the guardroom. Diepel, cap splashed red, was emerging like a wraith from the settling cloud of sand. Somewhere behind him, Monclaire heard the thin notes of a bugle as the General Alarm was sounded. And mingled with it was the crash of feet as

62

legionnaires ran out of the mess buildings and fell into files of three.

Diepel bawled over the row: 'They'll be here in a few minutes, *mon capitaine*.'

Monclaire noticed that the corporal's face was stained with tobacco juice as well as blood. Then he looked through the gap, the carnage-choked gap.

Out there, there was another cloud of dust. A long, advancing cloud created by a thousand galloping hooves. They were less than a mile off. They would be at the fort and thundering through the gap in under two minutes.

Unless . . .

Unless the gap could be held. Could be barricaded.

Monclaire made a swift assessment.

A heavy, water-cooled Maxim machine gun was mounted on each angle of the walls. Four of them in all. Devastating weapons, with a fire speed of sixty rounds a second.

He bawled at Diepel: 'The machine guns . . . every one of them must be down here and ready for action in a minute . . . '

Diepel disappeared into the confusion.

A sergeant appeared at Monclaire's side. Like Diepel, he was an old campaigner with the medal of the Bormone wars.

'Awaiting action orders, *mon capitaine.*'

It was a parade-ground voice. A voice without emotion.

'Detach two sections. They're to bring every item of furniture out of every compound building and pile it here in the gap. I'll dispose of the other men myself.'

Monclaire watched the sergeant move off at the double with forty men. That left about fifty others in the file.

In this moment every raw instinct told him to rush . . . to give a general order, any order, which would fill that awful gap with fifty rifles.

But he overcame the desire. He knew as well as any that an officer must never appear to be hurried. The greater the crisis, the more calm he must seem. Start to rush about, and the men start rushing too. The first result is chaos. The second is panic. The third, under these circumstances, is massacre.

He moved briskly, but not too briskly, to the file. He returned the salute of the senior NCO.

Then: 'Company, *attention!*'

They clicked into immobility.

'*Nombre.*'

They started to number from left to right. '*Un, deux, trois . . .* '

Nearly half of a precious minute had passed before the last man called, '*Cinquante.*'

'Numbers one to twenty-five . . . left turn . . . *Marche . . .* '

Half the file turned, marched and wheeled, so that when called to a halt they formed a quarter-circle covering the right-hand side of the gap.

The muffling thunder of cavalry hooves could be clearly heard.

Less than a minute left.

'Numbers twenty-six to fifty . . . right turn . . . *Marche . . .* '

A semi-circle about twenty yards deep was complete,

'*Fusil!*'

Fifty Lebels were raised to fifty

shoulders. And there was a hollow click as safety catches were moved forward.

From his position just outside the semi-circle, Monclaire looked first towards the Dylaks.

Less than three hundred yards off. They had concentrated so that they were approaching in a column hundreds of yards long. Their sabres were out. The thunder of hooves was no longer muffled. It was like a thousand drums and it seemed to torture the earth.

Only a few seconds now.

Monclaire looked towards the walls. The machine guns were not even dismantled yet. Sweating men were grouped round them. It had been expecting too much — far too much — to order them to be brought down within a minute. Freeing them from their emplacements was a difficult task. Manhandling them down the rampart steps, with their heavy tripods, condensers and water cans, would be even more complicated.

They would not be in position for at least three minutes. Probably more.

The miscalculation put Monclaire in an unexpected quandary.

His original plan had been based on the assumption that the machine guns would be ready before the Dylaks reached the gap. He would then have been able to switch at least two sections of the legionnaires to the walls, in case a secondary attack developed there.

But, as matters stood, the walls were practically unmanned. And they would remain so for some time, since every rifle would be needed down here.

Monclaire breathed a prayer. A prayer that the Dylaks would be so confident of storming the gap that they would not think of throwing grappling lines up to the ramparts. If they did, the few sentries on routine duty would be unable to put up more than a token resistance.

In a vague way, Monclaire was aware that a strange assortment of iron cots, wood tables, chairs, and even desks were being assembled at his side. They would be needed later — if they were needed at all.

A hundred yards off!

Those horsemen had the aspect of an irresistible force. Of blood and noise and cruelty at the maximum momentum.

Monclaire prepared to give the vital order.

And an odd thought flashed through his mind.

He whispered to himself: 'Nearly all my legionnaires are raw and untested . . . young, too . . . will they know how to fight . . . as their fathers fought . . . ?'

Yet even as he whispered, his eye was calculating the distance.

Sixty yards!

He glanced at his semi-circle. They were steady. Yes, they were steady enough. Yet this was a situation to try the nerves of any soldier. For an almost convulsive impulse to squeeze the trigger must be there. A rebellion of nature against a system which demanded that a man wait until the last excruciating moment before he defended himself.

They stood almost like toy troops, Lebels to their shoulders, left elbows well down, right eye following the lines of the leaf sights.

Monclaire's voice cut through the thunder of the hooves.

'Legionnaires . . . even numbers only . . . five rounds independent . . . fire!'

The stone walls accepted the sound waves of those twenty-five charges of exploding cordite and then threw them in an echo. But before the echo had died, the second explosions came. Then the third . . .

Noise and echo mingled in a wild cacophony.

But Monclaire was not aware of it. He was watching. Watching the Dylaks. Assessing the effect of the rounds. And he pursed his lips.

It was not good. Even at that close range, many of the shots were aimed too high. Others missed the leading horsemen and hit those following, where they caused the least confusion.

True, the momentum of the attack had abated a little, and the Dylaks were tending to fan out. But they were getting ever nearer the gap. And rifle fire of this kind would never keep them out.

'*Dieu!*' Monclaire shouted as rifles

were being reloaded. 'Keep your sights down . . . odd numbers . . . five rounds independent . . . fire!'

While the legionnaires with even numbers were pressing new clips into their magazines, the odd numbers opened up.

They were better — possibly because they had had the opportunity of observing the mistakes of their comrades. Their first three rounds were almost witheringly accurate. Horses reared and fell, trapping their riders. Other animals, crazed with terror, tried to turn away from the gate and caused pockets of whinnying, cursing confusion among those behind.

The final two rounds were less effective because many of the Dylaks were spreading out to the cover of the walls on either side.

The first assault had been held. But, as Monclaire knew, it had been the nearest of near things. And it was only the beginning.

For those horsemen who were still within sight had retreated to an area some eighty yards from the gap.

And there they were dismounting and taking cover behind a series of small dunes.

Monclaire guessed the reason. And his guess was confirmed when the legionnaires were swept by a scythe-like arc of fire. Fire from precision-built automatic rifles. From those Piets.

Three legionnaires standing slightly to Monclaire's left suddenly dropped their Lebels. One of them bent slowly forward, as if about to retrieve his weapon. Then he fell on his face and lay motionless. The two others performed a weird dance, spinning, sidestepping, then sinking slowly and simultaneously to the ground.

Nearer the walls, ten or eleven others had been hit, most of them wounded.

The Dylaks certainly had lost none of their traditional skill in war.

Their plan, Monclaire decided, was obvious. It was to drive the legionnaires to the cover of the walls — then rush the gap.

There was only one possible answer. The Dylaks must be pinned down by concentrated fire while the barricade was erected.

He looked behind him. The compound furniture had been assembled in a long, low ridge for easy handling. That sergeant was no fool. Monclaire called him over from where he was manhandling a trestle table.

'We must get this stuff into the gap immediately,' he said. 'We'll open blanket fire on the Dylaks. When that starts you must haul the stuff into position.'

The sergeant nodded. Monclaire turned away from him. He shouted: 'All numbers ... targets of opportunity ... fire!'

The stuttering of the Piets was submerged by the crash of the Lebels. Myriad fountains of sand rose and fell around the dunes where the Dylaks were taking cover. And the Dylak fire ceased ... for the moment.

In that moment the fatigue section started dragging the motley collection of objects into the gap between the walls.

Monclaire sweated as he watched.

For a new situation had developed.

Because legionnaires were now piling up the barricade, it had become impossible for the others to maintain the intensity of their blanket fire. If they had attempted to do so they would certainly have hit their own men.

It became a question of whether a rough barricade could be rushed up before the Dylaks realised and acted upon their advantage.

The Dylaks were slow. But that was not entirely their fault. Having been forced to earth under one withering blast of fire, they had no reason to believe that the same thing would not happen again if they raised their heads from behind the dunes. So, for the time being, they were content to remain inactive.

Gradually, as the barrier took shape, the tension eased.

It was not a formidable obstruction. In fact, it was in appearance more than slightly ridiculous. But it served its purpose. It made a sudden rush impossible. It gave cover to the defenders. And when the machine guns were in place . . .

Monclaire had forgotten about those Maxims.

He wheeled round to gaze at the ramparts. One legionnaire was halfway down the steps. He had a tripod over his shoulder, and a condenser and ammunition box in his hands. At the top, another man was staggering under the weight of the gun itself. Further along the ramparts, to the north and south, other legionnaire were bringing their dismantled guns.

Briefly, Monclaire indicated where the Maxims wen to be placed. One directly opposite the gap, but fifty yards back and almost under the compound buildings. Two others closer in and on either side. The fourth held in reserve outside any immediate angle of fire.

Monclaire watched the three-man teams go through the drill of mounting the Maxims. They did it well, he admitted. Almost with parade-ground crispness.

First, a man carried the tripod to the selected spot, jerked it up so that its splayed legs spread out, then secured them. After him came the legionnaire with the gun. He slapped it on the tripod and locked it there with a steel pin. Finally, the condenser and ammunition were brought up. The rubber tube was fixed to the underside of the corrugated barrel. The ammunition belt was fed into the magazine. The cocking hammer was jerked back and released twice.

And the Maxim .303 was ready to do a deal in sudden death.

None of the crews took more than fifty seconds to prepare. Which was good under any conditions.

Monclaire let go a sigh. For the time being, the gap was safe. Now — and only now — he could divert most of the garrison to their rightful place. To the ramparts.

He heard a yell above the intermittent firing. It came from above and to his left.

Something was glittering on the top of the west ramparts. Something like a great, bright, slithering snake. It was joined by others on either side of it. Then more still.

A legionnaire — that American legionnaire — was trying to lever them off with the butt of his rifle. He could not. So he leaned perilously forward and fired direct down the outside of the wall.

The grappling hooks were up.

Like nightmarish monkeys, the Dylaks were swarming up the ropes to storm the almost undefended ramparts.

★ ★ ★

Up to now, Rex had been no more than a spectator. And that was not a role that he ever filled gladly.

After being nearly blown off the ledge he had been compelled, trigger finger involuntarily twitching, to watch the battle of the gap. It gave him a feeling of helpless superfluity.

According to standing orders, he should have paid little attention to the fighting. He should have been watching his ramparts. But few men would have been able to observe such punctilious restraint. Certainly not a man with Rex's volatile Brooklyn temperament.

He cursed richly. He stamped like a restless horse. But it was no use. It seemed that he was merely to watch while vital issues were decided.

Once or twice he glanced at Legionnaire Anoti. The Italian showed no similar desire to become embroiled in the fighting. In fact, from his position on the north wall he looked mightily relieved to be out of it.

And on occasion Rex glanced over his own ramparts. But there had been little he could do from there.

During the Dylak attack he had fired a few rounds, but the angle had made accurate shooting almost impossible, and he soon gave that up.

He was confronted with the same impossibility when some of the Dylaks took cover directly under the wall.

He was ruminating heavily when he saw the first grappling hook.

It rose several feet above the wall and seemed to pause for a moment in mid-air. A wicked three-pronged piece of metal attached to a thick, knotted rope. Then it crashed onto the inside top edge of the ramparts, slithered, and took grip. Immediately, the rope became taut. Rex knew why it was taut. The Dylaks were already climbing.

He bawled something. He did not know what it was. Just something. And, far below, he saw Monclaire look towards him.

Distantly and vaguely, he heard a series of shouted orders from the compound. Help was on the way. But when would it arrive? Meantime, he was alone on the west ramparts with the Dylaks swarming up.

Other grappling hooks had wavered in the air and taken grip. It was impossible to free them.

Simultaneously, five Dylaks appeared over different parts of the ramparts. They flung themselves astride the stonework while dragging free their short knives. Each had a Piet slung over his shoulder.

They were followed by others. Suddenly the stone of the ramparts became invisible under the mass of grey robes.

He heard a stutter of shots and a shriek from the north wall. Anoti was twisting down through space, tearing at his crimson throat.

From either side, the Dylaks were advancing on Rex. They were going to use their knives because, at such close range, they might kill each other with their Piets.

Rex braced himself.

And he said: 'Jeez . . . was I complaining about not getting any action . . . ?'

5

The Last Signal

Back to Captain Monclaire . . .

It was minutes that did it. Minutes that defeated him. Two, perhaps three of them. Nothing in the passage of time. Everything in the passage of human events. For if the Dylaks had delayed their attack on the wall just a hundred and twenty seconds longer, then the ramparts would have been manned.

And the scales would have been weighed in favour of the legionnaires, for the man behind the fortification is nearly always in a stronger position than the one trying to storm it.

But the ramparts were undefended — undefended except for one sentry on each of the four walls. And the man defending the north wall was already a casualty.

Within a few moments the Dylaks

would be in the compound. The inevitable result would be butchery.

It was here that Monclaire called upon a lifetime of military experience. He did not attempt the obvious. He did not attempt to send the legionnaires rushing up the narrow wall steps where they would be cut down from the top by the Piets.

Instead, he gave an order which formed the men in a circle surrounding the compound buildings and facing the walls. From that position, they had a clear field of fire at the teeming Dylaks on the ramparts.

He caught a glimpse of a lone uniform struggling amid a mass of robes and the glitter of knives. He thought: 'It's the American . . . '

Then he gave the order.

'Legionnaires . . . five rounds . . . independent . . . fire!'

★   ★   ★

Back to Rex.

A man doesn't think when he quivers

81

on the abyss of eternity. The animal instinct takes over. That was how it was with Rex.

And, as is often the case, the instinctive reaction was the right one.

The nearest Dylak was on Rex's left side. He was tall, and had his five-inch stabbing knife held low, poised for an upwards slash at Rex's stomach.

Rex had his Lebel at waist level. As he squeezed the trigger the rifle twisted viciously under the uncontrolled recoil. The Dylak pirouetted and fell across the ramparts. Then, from the same technically incorrect position, Rex jerked back the bolt, slid a new cartridge into the breech, and fired at the Arab on the other side. The Dylak slumped forward and died with his face pressed against the stone of the ledge.

The result was a moment of breathing space.

A moment in which Rex realised that he held one slender advantage. He could shoot. The Dylaks could not. A cross-shot from one Dylak would certainly hit another on the opposite side of Rex.

But the lull and the advantage did not last long.

It was ended by a Dylak who had just reached the top of the rope. This warrior immediately realised the situation. He did not attempt to join the others on the ledge. Instead, he remained kneeling on the ramparts while he unslung his Piet. From that angle there was no chance of hitting anyone — except Rex.

Rex saw the Dylak as he was raising the Piet to his robed shoulder.

He again pressed the trigger of the Lebel. And the result was extraordinary.

The Dylak rose from his kneeling position, dropping his Piet at the same time. He stood on the ramparts, little more than the whites of his eyes showing, and half his neck blown away. Then he projected himself at Rex.

Rex had neither the time nor the space in which to get out of the way. He twisted slightly sideways as the body struck him. The two crashed on to the ledge. The Dylak must have died in mid-air, for he did not move after that.

But he had served his turn. Arabs on

either side rushed at Rex's prostrate form.

He managed to get to his knees. But he was helpless. He knew he was helpless. His Lebel had slid out of reach, and in any event there was not the room in which to use it. And already the Dylaks were over him. He sensed rather than saw their knives rising, preparatory to a downward thrust between his shoulders.

From far, far off, he heard the voice of Monclaire. It was giving an order. An order which should have meant something to him. But it had no meaning now, as he waited for the steel to burn and twist through his flesh.

No meaning at all — until he heard the echoing crash of musketry from the compound.

Until he heard the harp-like whine of slugs which had missed their target.

Until he heard the sudden retching for breath and the animal moans of those who had not escaped.

Until he realised that no knives had ripped into him, and that those who had held them were now crumbling to the ledge or rolling off it.

Instinct . . .

Again, Rex worked by instinct.

His right hand groped and closed round the breech block of his Lebel. His eyes assessed the distance to the steps. They were close. No more than eight yards. And most of the Arabs who had stood in the way were now dead. Or too confused for the moment to offer serious resistance. The main risk came from the bullets of the legionnaires. But that was a risk that had to be accepted.

Half-crawling, half-running, Rex made for those steps. An Arab, bleeding fatally from the main wrist artery, tried to knife him with his good hand. Rex did not need to do anything about that. The man died with his knife suspended in the air.

A second volley came from the compound.

For a moment the air seemed solid. Solid with hot, spinning lead. The stonework streaked, cracked, and chipped a few inches in front of Rex. If he'd been moving just a little faster . . .

Maybe the legionnaires could not see him clearly? Maybe it would be safer to stand up and make a direct run for it?

He acted on the decision almost before he had made it.

And, as he got to his feet, the third volley came. But the shots were well clear of him. They had recognised him! They were giving covering fire so he could get down those goddam steps!

He felt more confident now. Anyway, more confident than he had felt for a heck of a time!

The steps were under his boots. Steps to safety . . . no, not safety . . . but steps that led to his friends. At least he would die among those he knew . . .

He joined the legionnaires in the compound as they were firing the fifth volley.

★   ★   ★

When neither side had gained a decisive advantage, the Staff College (in their lectures) described the position as being one of Static Attrition.

To Monclaire, that seemed to be the situation at the moment.

The gap was secured. It would need a division of infantry with mortars to storm that narrowing opening against the firepower of the heavy machine guns.

The attack on the walls had been contained.

Certainly the garrison had temporarily lost the use of the ramparts, and that had been a serious blow. But on the other hand, the Dylaks had not made any use of them. Those who had survived the Lebel fire had retreated down the ropes to the other side. And now the ledges were littered with dead and dying.

That was the short-term view.

An appreciation which merely embraced the next few hours.

But when night came . . .

There was total darkness for almost three hours before the moon rose. In that time, the Dylaks might be able to mount another attack on the walls which, cloaked in invisibility, would be difficult to repel.

However, fears apart, the first move must be to get as many men as possible back on these ramparts.

But how many?

It was a difficult question in manpower distribution. Men needed rest, needed food. All of them could not remain there all the time.

Monclaire called for a count of his effective strength. It was ninety-four. There had been twenty-three casualties — eleven dead and twelve wounded, now in the sick bay under the care of the medical officer.

Monclaire decided to fall back on the well-tested system of 'third about'. One-third on duty, two-thirds off, in periods of three hours on and six for rest.

Those off-duty would eat and sleep in full equipment. He gave the order to Lieutenant Gina.

He was no longer pallid. There was a flush of virility about him. That adolescent uncertainty of his had gone, too. He received Monclaire's orders with a decisive crispness.

And as Monclaire went to the wireless room he thought: '*Dieu!* Gina has a right to be pleased. He has faced death for the first time. And he has found that he is not

88

a coward. It is a good moment for any soldier . . . '

There was something odd, ridiculous in fact, about the inside of the compound buildings. The stone corridors, the doors — they were the same as before.

It was difficult to believe that everything was not normal. Difficult, in this atmosphere, to credit that Fort Valeau was at this moment encircled by crazed Dylaks. That the gates had been blown up by three fanatics, that there had been a fiendish battle to hold the resulting gap, that the walls had so nearly been stormed . . .

The sense of unreality was even more pronounced in the wireless room. The same rather intellectual-looking Polish legionnaire was there behind his tiny table. The same bewildering array of valves and wires in front of him. The same headphones and Morse-tapping key.

The Pole jerked upright and stood at attention. He looked indignant.

'Well?' Monclaire asked.

'*Capitaine* . . . a little time ago they

came in here and wanted to take my chair and table.'

His voice shook with umbrage. And Monclaire found himself smiling.

'You're fortunate. Your privileged position enabled you to retain some of the comforts. None of the rest of us has either a chair or a table at all.'

The Pole looked shocked. Isolated in this cubbyhole, he could have had little idea of what was going on. But his plaint destroyed that atmosphere. Suddenly Monclaire realised that the buildings were not the same. Except for here, there was no furniture in them. They had been stripped naked.

Monclaire picked up a pencil from the table. He drew a cypher pad towards him and wrote:

Priority Absolute. To Commandant's Secretary, Dini Sadazi. From Commanding Officer, Fort Valeau. Under attack by strong force well-armed Dylak tribesmen. Gates breached. Situation critical. Advise whether air strike is possible.

He read his words carefully. It was the last sentence which was vital. If planes could strafe the Dylaks, the position would be relieved immediately. But could they? He was not clear on that point, for the liaison between the French African Air Force and the Foreign Legion was notoriously poor. He knew there was an Air Force base at Oran. But that was eight hundred miles off. A sixteen-hundred-mile round trip. Only heavy bombers could manage that — and they might not be available. And, even if they were, how long would it take before the take-off order was finally given?

Monclaire mentally groaned at the prospect. He could visualise it all so clearly.

First Sadazi would refer his signal to Algiers. At Algiers, they would probably call a staff conference to discuss it. Then, if all went well, a request would be sent to the Air Officer Commanding at Oran.

Monclaire had little hope as he flipped the cypher pad over and said: 'Send it.'

He watched the operator put headphones over a close-shaven head. He watched him start to tap out the recognition signal on the key.

It was repeated several times. Then, faintly, he heard Sadazi replying in a series of long and short buzzes. They were giving the code of acknowledgement 'PR', which was the signal to proceed with the message.

At that moment, something compelled Monclaire to look up at the narrow window high over the desk.

He was in time to see it disintegrate into slivers. Almost at the same time, he heard a raw crash from immediately outside. It was accompanied by the slapping of hard material against the thick wall. The room trembled.

A second's pause.

Then another similar explosion. And a third. And with them, the sound of men running and the shout of orders.

Monclaire did not have to see the projectiles to know what they were. He recognised them by the noise they made. They were .240 grenades. Normally they were used as hand grenades. But, when fixed to a muzzle cup, they could be fired from a rifle. And, because of the range, that was obviously the way these were being fired.

The Pole pulled his earphones off his head and stared blankly at the broken glass.

There was an ugly rasp in Monclaire's voice.

'Put those on and send the message. Hurry!'

The operator mumbled something in his own tongue and resumed tapping the key. He tapped the same letter sequence several times. Then he half-rose to check the wire plugs.

That done, he turned helplessly to Monclaire.

He did not need to speak. It was obvious. For the time being, at least, a grenade had put the wireless out of action.

Strained nerves made Monclaire get near to snarling at the man. 'Don't stand about. Can you repair it?'

'I don't know yet, *capitaine*.'

'Then find out. And if you can mend it, do so. Then let me know.'

He strode out, needlessly slamming the door.

Outside, it was largely as he had anticipated. As well as Piet automatic rifles, the Dylaks had grenade cups to attach to them. The ghastly result was that grenades were easily clearing the barricade and the walls and exploding in the compound.

Monclaire knew that nothing — absolutely nothing — was so demoralising to men as being exposed to the hot hell of such weapons. The screeching fragmentations almost always result in uncanny wounds. They took away any part of a man's body with the neat certainty of a surgeon's knife.

And that had happened already.

It had happened inside the barricade.

The crews of two of the machine guns were huddled and inert. One gun lay on its side. The other, by some incongruous miracle, had been blown upside down, and its tripod pointed to the sky like the legs of a huge spider.

The two other machine guns were untouched. But the men who had manned them were gone.

Monclaire stared at the abandoned weapons. Stared with eyes that did not want to believe what they saw.

'*De mal en pis!*' he whispered to himself. 'They ran . . . they fled. My old legionnaires . . . they would not have done that!'

Yet, as he uttered the bitter recrimination, he wondered whether it was true.

Could any soldiers be expected to remain in the open while bombarded by fragmentation grenades? And these young legionnaires were facing something that had never confronted the veterans. They were facing tribesmen who, somehow, had secured the most modern of infantry weapons.

It was the stunning nature of the fact itself that momentarily deprived Monclaire of the power of action. But it was only momentary.

The barricade was unguarded. And, with the grenades being used, there was no hope of holding it. At any moment the

Dylaks would break through.

Lieutenant Gina was at his side. Monclaire felt glad of the fact. He would have made a good officer after all, would Gina. Would have . . . He felt sorry for him. Almost paternal.

'We can't fight the grenades, Gina. That's impossible. You realise that?'

Gina looked astonished.

'You mean we're going to . . . '

'*Non!* We do not surrender. It's better to die here than become playthings for the Dylak women and their torture knives. But before we die we'll leave our mark, Gina. They'll remember the garrison of Valeau. Recall the men from the ramparts. We're going to let the Dylaks have the compound. We'll fight from inside the buildings.'

It was, Monclaire knew, the only chance of prolonging the resistance.

The buildings were in a single square block. It would make a fort within a fort. And no part of it was isolated from the other. No part of it at all. Except the punishment cell . . .

The punishment cell!

A legionnaire was in there.

Monclaire remembered the Englishman. The powerfully built, strangely cultured Legionnaire Havers, whom he had sentenced the previous night.

According to strict orders, he should have been freed at the immediate start of the emergency. But no one had had time to think of a routine matter like that. He must be released immediately.

He looked for an NCO.

And, as he was looking, a grenade exploded thirty yards ahead of Monclaire.

The pieces of hot shrapnel flew out laterally. Some of them bit deep into the compound walls. Some of them hit legionnaires who were already retreating down the west wall steps.

And one of them — a piece no bigger than a large button — hit Monclaire on the front centre of his hat.

He stood for a while, motionless. A look of utter weariness enveloped his face. Then he dropped on his back and remained there. Like a man asleep.

★   ★   ★

But Rex had also remembered Pete Havers. He had remembered him when the first grenades came over. He, with the rest of Corporal Diepel's section, had been ordered to rest and eat. They had just got into the main mess room when the new explosions were heard.

Rex was no strategist. He was not even a tactician. But he had been in enough action to know that nothing could now prevent the Dylaks storming the gap. And the first building they would reach would be the isolated punishment cell. With Pete in it!

He looked quickly around.

The others were producing their iron mess tins. A fatigue party was dropping iron rations into each of them. Three biscuits, a stick of dried dates, plus a cup of water.

Rex picked up his rifle.

No one saw him move out of the mess room door, down the short corridor and into the open compound.

As he emerged, a grenade fell almost at his feet. Instinctively, he darted back into the cover of the building — yet he knew as he did so that he would be too late.

He was not too late.

The grenade did not burst until several clear seconds after he had darted behind the wall. The Dylaks, it seemed, were using delayed action fuses as well as contact detonators.

When the burst had spent itself Rex emerged again.

The corridor gave on to the east side of the fort — the side which up till now had been comparatively quiet. He turned to the left and, keeping close to the wall, he made for the punishment cell.

He reached it inside a minute.

He skirted round to the door. This door faced the now unguarded barricade.

Rex bawled through: 'Hey, for Pete's sake what d'you want a stay in there for!'

It was a weak pun, but he could seldom resist using it.

Pete's imperturbable face appeared at the barred window.

He said: 'It's becoming a trifle tiresome in here, old man. In fact, there's no joy in it. No joy at all.'

'I figured that out myself. That's why

I'm here. I'm gonna shoot the god-damned lock in, so keep clear of the door.'

Rex raised his Lebel. At that moment a peculiar cracking and scraping noise came from some distance behind him. He glanced over his shoulder. And he felt his chest muscles contract.

The barricade was moving inwards and falling apart.

The Dylaks outside were pressing on it and dismembering it.

That fantastic conglomeration of odd-ments could not possibly serve as an obstruction for more than a few further seconds. Then the Dylaks would be through. And Rex realised the discom-forting fact that he would be the first living person they would see as they burst into the compound. Unless he and Pete got away mighty fast.

The punishment cell itself was built of brown stone, like the rest of the fort. Its door was of four-inch teak, secured by a double lock. One lock in the centre, and the other slightly above eye-level, near the top.

Rex decided to deal with the higher lock first.

From a range of less than three feet he sighted on the massive keyhole and squeezed the trigger.

He found the result astounding.

The lock seemed to quiver and jump in its seating, then fold over on itself like a slab of soft rubber. But it was not destroyed. It was still holding the door.

Rex grunted and said something forceful. He was beginning to appreciate that blowing in a lock is not such an easy process as is generally thought.

Pete's smooth voice came through the bars.

'My dear fellow, if you really intend to blow that thing in, you'll only do it if you shoot under and upwards. And don't stand back. Press the muzzle against it.'

This time, Rex did just that. He pressed the muzzle of the Lebel against the bottom edge of the lock. Again he fired. This time, the result was less dramatic but more satisfactory. The entire mechanism fell away from the door.

He jerked back the rifle bolt, then

whipped it forward. As he did so, he glanced over his shoulder. There was nothing to comfort him there. The last remnants of the barricade were being torn and pushed away. Behind it, the feverishly working Dylaks could be clearly seen.

Rex got to work on the lower lock.

This time, the slug ricocheted. It behaved like a mad hornet, seeming to twist back in mid-flight and skim along the outer barrel of the Lebel. Rex felt a brush of air as it flashed past his hand. But it had done its work. The door was swinging open.

And Pete suddenly appeared through it. His finely cast features were twisted into a sardonic smile. He wore no cap and his fair hair had partly flopped over his eyes. He brushed it away. 'This,' he said, 'is not an occasion which calls for undue delay. It occurs to me that the natives are hostile. We had better depart at speed.'

Rex did not answer. He turned to go.

Then he saw Monclaire.

It had been his intention to return by

the same route by which he had arrived — along the quieter side, where the compound buildings would give cover from the Dylaks.

It was pure chance that, in turning, he noticed the huddled figure.

Even at that distance of two hundred yards there was no mistaking it. No mistaking the silver-braided cap, the gold-and-silver shoulder epaulet.

He touched Pete's arm and pointed.

No words were necessary. They ran to where Monclaire lay.

In the ordinary way, Monclaire would have been seen before this by the legionnaires who were retreating from the ramparts. But, by a strange stroke of fortune, he had fallen behind the angle of his own office window, and was thus concealed from anyone in the vicinity of the wall steps.

Rex prepared to lift him. But Pete said: 'Wait a moment. Let's see what the damage is. If you start hurling him about you may kill him — if he's not killed already.'

Pete made a quick examination, long

and sensitive hands probing for wounds. Rex found himself wondering about those hands. They were not the sort of hands that you usually saw in the Legion . . .

Pete stood up. He held Monclaire's cap and pointed to the badge. It was scratched and flattened.

'The captain's a lucky man. If it hadn't been for that badge he would be dead. As it is, I think he's only concussed. Let's get him in.'

They carried him into the compound just as the garrison started to lock and bar the doors. And as shrieking Dylaks finally burst through the barricade.

6

The Lash

Some tragedies are inevitable. Neither the courage, the wit, nor the unyielding spirit of men can avoid them. Inevitable tragedies are those which are a logical sequel to related events. The fall of Fort Valeau was just such a sequel.

As a permanent fortress, the compound buildings were untenable. But Monclaire had calculated with good reason that they could be held for some days at least.

And probably they would have been held thus long — if Monclaire had been available to conduct the defence.

But he was not. During the whole of those blood-laden hours between late afternoon and evening, he lay semi-conscious in the sick bay.

Lieutenant Gina did his best. And it was a good best. But men react to officers according to the way they feel about them. They respected Monclaire. Although they would never have thought of saying so, they knew he had a masterly grip of infantry tactics. They knew, too, that if anyone could extricate them from this inferno, it was Monclaire. Yes — they had cursed him often enough. But in the hour of trial they turned to him. Not to Gina.

Gina was an uncertain quantity. Those who had had time to notice admitted that he had conducted himself well in the fighting. Surprisingly well. But even to them there was still that atmosphere of hesitant immaturity about him. It might, in truth, have disappeared in recent hours. But in the minds of the legionnaires it was still there because it was still remembered. Gina was a substitute. And substitutes would not do.

So, subconsciously, they found themselves doubting his orders. Wondering if they were the right ones. Wondering if Monclaire would have done the same thing . . .

It was a fatal attitude for any troops to take. But a completely natural one.

The Dylaks did not waste time. They spent the minimum of time regrouping inside the fort walls. Then they attacked the compound buildings at every point simultaneously.

And their system of attack had something of the efficiency of an army trained in street fighting.

First the grenades were aimed at the windows. Most, it is true, missed and exploded harmlessly outside the walls. But some smashed through the glass . . .

When that happened, the rooms affected were areas of utter death and chaos. The fortunate ones died immediately. The less fortunate screamed as they looked at the raw stumps where, just a second before, limbs had been . . .

Those who by some miracle escaped physical harm were often too dazed, too demoralized, to resist further. It was almost a relief to be bound and kicked by their Dylak captors.

For, each time a grenade exploded inside a window, the Dylaks followed it within moments.

The smaller rooms, including the

administrative building, were at either end. Therefore it was natural that they fell first, for in the more confined space the grenades had a greater effect. Within two hours of the start of the second attack, Lieutenant Gina was left with only some thirty men and control of the main mess hall, the sick bay (wherein the medical officer was still performing prodigious feats under conditions of unimaginable horror), and the magazine — which was below ground level and ran directly beneath.

The mess hall and the sick bay had escaped serious damage because of a suggestion made by Legionnaire Havers.

Normally, the obvious move against the grenades would have been to board up the windows. But there was no material with which to do so. Almost all the suitable material had been used for the barricade.

Keeping well below window level, Pete crawled to where Gina was squatting, pistol in hand, in the centre of the hall.

'I suggest, Lieutenant, that we use the floorboards to protect the windows.'

Rex heard the suggestion. It surprised him. Not the words themselves, but the way they were spoken. They were not the tones of a legionnaire addressing an officer. They were the tones of one officer to another. Calm, casual, confident . . .

But Gina did not appear to notice anything. And it was to his credit that he acted upon the suggestion immediately. Within a few minutes, boarding was torn up and lashed against the window frames.

It delayed the final collapse. But it was only a delay. The Dylaks eventually solved the problem quite simply. They ignored the windows. They ceased attacking altogether. There was a sudden, unreal silence.

Rex, peering through an aperture in the window boards, saw the reason. Dylaks were emerging from the already captured fort kitchens. They were carrying cans of paraffin oil, used for the stoves and the lamps.

They were going to set fire to the compound.

It was then that Lieutenant Gina

decided to take a chance. The only chance.

He decided to surrender.

*   *   *

It's easy to criticise. Easy to say that it was death, anyway, to surrender to the Dylaks. So why not fight on? Why not make a last heroic charge out of the compound and be killed in the open?

Or something equally fatuous.

In hard fact, Gina was right.

He was incapable of further effective resistance. And he had not only the handful of men around him to think of. He also had to think of those who lay wounded in the sick bay. No death that the Dylaks could contrive could be more horrible than that of helpless men being shrivelled to death in a vast oven.

And there was a chance — just a chance — that the Dylaks would not slay them. True, the precedent of the relief company was against the prospect. But any chance was better than none.

The legionnaires understood that. They

had had enough. They had fought to a standstill and they could not fight any more. That was all that could be asked of soldiers. The only people who are always prepared to fight to the end without reason are inevitably civilians in armchairs.

Gina himself pulled down the boarding from one of the windows. And from it he fluttered a filthy handkerchief that had once been white.

A few minutes later, he led his legionnaires out of the building, and into the fort yard where a great circle of Dylaks awaited them.

And the circle closed round them, like the tightening of a human noose.

Sabres flicked at them. With their short knives the Dylaks made obscene gestures towards them. They laughed at them. In their sibilant dialect they jeered at them.

Rex thought: 'Buddy — this is curtains.'

Pete thought: 'I'm not counting on a long and prosperous future.'

Corporal Diepel thought: 'They're going to carve our bellies out.'

Then Monclaire appeared.

He came out of the door leading from the sick bay. He pushed through the Dylaks. And somehow they parted to make way for him. He made a strange yet faintly glorious figure, did Captain Monclaire in that moment. His uniform had obviously been dragged hurriedly on, for several buttons were unfastened. His cap sat unfittingly on the bandages which swathed his forehead. He had obviously only recovered consciousness recently, for his face had a yellowish pallor, and (despite the increasing cool of the evening) driblets of sweat were running down his cheeks and chin.

He reached the side of Gina. And as he did so there was a sudden stiffening of the spirit of the legionnaires.

The *capitaine* was back! The *capitaine* would know what to do!

It was child-like faith. The faith that all frightened men feel towards natural leaders. A manifestation of an inborn desire for assurance and support.

Monclaire's voice gave force to their

belief. It was in contrast to his appearance. It had vibrancy, strength. Authority, too.

'Who is in charge of this rabble?'

He disdained the Dylak dialect. He spoke in French, knowing that most Dylaks were well versed in the tongue.

Silence. An absolute epitome of silence.

The sabres ceased to flick and wave. The gestures with the short knives were stilled. This was the insult absolute, coming from the defeated commander to the victorious enemy.

Perhaps, when the Dylaks had recovered, they would have ripped Monclaire to bits. And done the same with the legionnaires around him. And then set to work on the wounded in the sick bay. Perhaps . . . There was no means of knowing. For while his words were still working their stunning effect there was a disturbance from the back of the vast assembly.

Rex, because he was the tallest of the legionnaires, saw them first. And his amazement expressed itself in a quick, highly audible intake of breath.

Pushing through the warriors were two figures on horseback.

The animals themselves were enough to hold the attention.

Bridles of shimmering silver swathed their sleek and slim heads. The horns of their saddles were gold-tipped and inset with richly flashing ruby stones. Magnificent thoroughbreds — and magnificently equipped.

But their riders offered an even more unusual spectacle. One of them was a slender young man with brown-hued features which suggested a ferocious cat. Under a blue brocaded turban, his thin lips were pulled back in an expression which could equally have been a smile or a snarl. His eyes were weirdly feline, too. Green. Green in a land where the only colour was brown. And his robes were mingled blues and reds, velvets and silks in lush profusion.

The other . . .

The other was a woman.

Her robes were as magnificent as those of the man at her side. And she had his startlingly green eyes. A suggestion of his felinity, of his cruelty. But there was beauty, too, in that face of hers. A proud, arrogant beauty that held and compelled.

And she was white.

★ ★ ★

The Dylaks held back until the two were in the centre of the circle and directly in front of Monclaire. Then, as though carefully rehearsed, they sheathed swords and knives and salaamed. And they called one word which filled the gathering night.

'Zanal!'

The brown-faced man and the white woman looked down on Monclaire. If Monclaire felt any surprise (which he must have done), he did not show it. He returned their gaze. And even in that moment he did not seem to lose an iota of his authority, of his capacity to dominate.

The woman transferred her glance from Monclaire to the legionnaires. The huddled group of weary and helpless men seemed to amuse her. Her lips, full and red, parted in a semi-smile. She twirled an ivory-hilted riding whip.

It was completely typical of Monclaire that he did not wait to be addressed. He spoke first. It was substantially a repetition of his previous question.

'Are you in charge of this rabble?'

He had half-turned his back on the woman and was looking at the man.

But it was the woman who answered him. She did so in an unexpected way.

She eased her mount forward a few yards. Then, almost before it was possible to comprehend what was happening, she slashed the riding whip down and across Monclaire's cheek.

It was a three-thong knotted leather whip. A cruel thing to use on an animal. Its effect on the bare flesh of a man was hideous.

It cracked in the air like a shot from a small pistol. It seemed to stick for a moment against Monclaire's face. Then it fell away, as though satisfied with its own infamy.

Monclaire did not move under the impact. He did not even flinch.

But his face . . .

Three long furrows of raw flesh and blood stretched from his right ear to the angle of his chin.

Only those who stood closest to Monclaire heard his battle for breath. Heard the faint retching within his lungs. But Pete, who was closest of all, heard it. So did Rex. So did Diepel.

The blood started to ooze and spread. It turned the injured side of Monclaire's face into a crimson horror. But he smiled. It was against every law of nature, every law of logic, that smile. It was inexplicable. But many things about many people are inexplicable. Some men just *can*.

And he said quietly: 'Madame has long claws . . . '

She drew back her lovely, satanic mouth, showing pearl-white teeth. And the thongs descended again.

But this time they did not touch Monclaire. The whip was arrested in mid-flight.

Two strong hands had closed over the whip handle. Slender, but strong hands. The hands of Legionnaire Pete Havers.

He twisted the whip. It would have been sufficient to dislodge it from the grasp of most people. But the woman, too, had strength. Strength and tenacity. Leaning forward in the saddle, she tried to pull it away from him.

For a moment she swayed. Then the two of them — the white women in Dylak robes and the English legionnaire — crashed together on to the ground.

She fell beneath him. Pete, for the briefest of periods, felt a strange and contradictory sensation. A sensation he had not experienced for many long months.

He felt her slim, young, supple body. Sensed the warmth of it. The suggestion of it. The beauty of it. And her face. As she writhed, it momentarily brushed against his face. Small and white. Her turban had come away. Long, raven-black hair splayed onto the yellow sand . . .

Then it was all over. It passed like the glimpse of a strange heaven amid the torments of a wild hell.

Rough arms were pulling him up. Feet were kicking him. Rifle butts and sword hilts bruising him. He felt the blessed relief of fading senses.

But the torment stopped. It stopped at the command of the woman. She stood opposite Pete. She spoke. A cat hissing.

She was saying: 'You will stay with us. All of you will stay with us. And before you die, you will know pain such as few men have endured. And you will learn things, too. Things of which the government of France do not dream . . . '

7

In the Shadows

Their hands were bound and they were loosely roped together. Then they were driven into what had been the wireless room of the fort. It was now a bleak shambles of smashed glass and spewing wire. To get more than twenty men into that tiny place was a nominal impossibility But the Dylaks achieved it. The prisoners stood so close against each other that breathing became a matter of pain and movement impossible.

The door was locked on them. Guards were outside it, and outside the window.

They scarcely spoke, those captives. Under such conditions speech was a physical effort. And, in any case, their bewilderment, their exhaustion, their fear . . . they could not be phrased in words.

Monclaire?

He stood against a wall while those

nearest tried to ease the pressure against him. Blood had dried and crusted on his cheek. His head bandage had fallen off, revealing a massive blue swelling. His eyes were weary and ill.

Rex?

He was under the small window. There, he could get some of the clean air. There, he contrived to recall the past . . .

Pete?

He was in the centre of the ghastly, grunting crush. No place for him to lean, save against those pressed against him. His legs, his arms, his shoulders, his head — they all ached because of the beating he had received. But he was not aware of the pain. He was not in Fort Valeau at all. He was back in England. Back with his county regiment in a small garrison town.

It had happened by the merest chance. Most really big events start that way. They are seldom the result of deliberate calculation.

The cool sweetness of spring was in the air when Lieutenant Pete Havers had dismissed his platoon on that Wednesday morning and strolled into the mess for a pink gin before lunch.

All had seemed completely right with the world. Nothing could go wrong. He had two years' seniority in his rank. In another couple of years, with ordinary luck, he would get his third pip. He got on well with his fellow officers and, so far as it was possible for a subaltern to judge, he seemed to be making a fair impression on the colonel. And he liked the life. For him, it was the only conceivable life. Just as it had been for his father. And his father's father. Public school — Sandhurst — the regiment. It was automatic. The only difference in his case was that he had to depend almost entirely on his pay. The family resources were not what they had been. But that did not bother him much. His tastes were modest enough.

The mess bar had been fairly full that morning.

The adjutant, beatific and important, was entertaining some visitors from a nearby Armoured Corps regiment.

Pete was asked to join the party.

It was a good party. A first-class

mid-day drinking session. And Pete was able to enjoy it because he had signed the short-leave book, and was not on duty again until the following day.

He was not drunk when he got into his small sports car to drive to London. But he was not sober either.

It was the old gentleman's fault. He ambled onto the road from behind a parked van. Pete had no chance at all, even though he was travelling quite slowly.

He stood trial for manslaughter.

The judge took copious notes while evidence was given on the amount of drink he'd had. And the jury was impressed.

The result was six months' imprisonment.

And a wrecked career.

When he came out, Pete got a statement from his bank. He deducted the cost of third-class travel to Marseilles. He sent a cheque for the entire balance to the dependants of the man he had killed.

And Lieutenant Havers, of a famous

English county regiment, underwent a drastic metamorphosis. He became Legionnaire Havers . . .

Diepel?

He was crushed against the door. And he was worrying vastly. It was a question of chewing tobacco. He had only one small plug left . . .

Diepel consoled himself in the end with typical Scandinavian materialism. He decided that his tobacco would in all probability more than last his remaining span of life.

It was towards midnight when they heard the horror.

They heard screams. Piercing, trembling, terror-laden expressions of fear and agony. They lasted for less than two minutes. And they came from the fort sick bay, where the wounded were.

All of them in that room knew what had happened. But none dared to speak of it. None except Diepel. He put his mouth to the door, and in bad French he bawled: 'You swine . . . what have you done . . . ?'

There was a scuffle from outside. The

door was unlocked and opened. The magnificently brocaded figure who had been greeted with the name 'Zanal' stood in the threshold. He was wearing that cat-like smile.

And he said: 'You ought to be grateful to us. We have put your wounded comrades out of all pain.'

He paused. The smile faded. He looked at the hot, congested mass as though making a careful assessment. Then he added: 'You, all of you, could be more fortunate. It is a matter for each of you to decide for himself. But it cannot be discussed here. You will meet Tania and me in a few minutes.'

He turned. He seemed to dissolve away amid the shadows.

And there was a heavy, thoughtful silence after he left. Most of the legionnaires had understood his fluent French. But the common question was phrased by Rex. He asked: 'Who's Tania? Is it that witch with the whip?'

'I don't think there is much doubt of that, *mon legionnaire*.'

From his position under the window,

Rex managed to twist round slightly so he could see Monclaire.

'She's white . . . as white as anyone here. I don't get it.'

Monclaire smiled faintly at the idiom.

'None of us, as you say, get it. But I think we'll all have the explanation before long.'

Corporal Diepel spat out some tobacco juice. It was intended for the floor. But he had overlooked the fact that in that crowded place no floor space was available. The brown liquid was absorbed by the well-cut breeches of Lieutenant Gina. Gina did not notice. It could scarcely have made any difference if he had.

Then Diepel said: 'Mon *capitaine*, what do you think that Dylak meant when he said we could be more fortunate than . . . than the legionnaires who were wounded?'

'It could mean any of many things. There is no means of knowing. But again — I think we'll have the answer soon.'

★ ★ ★

126

Ten minutes later they were escorted out of the tiny room.

Still roped loosely together and with their hands secured, they were taken along the battle-scarred corridors and out into the night air.

The moon was riding high and big. It gave a stark light to a mixture of the familiar and the fantastic.

There were the great walls of Valeau. Massive and permanent. A monument to the military might of France.

There, at their backs, was the compound. Save for the smashed windows, little other damage could be seen. It, too, appeared the same as ever. Squat and compact. And dominated by the towering ninety-foot steel flag pole. But no Tricolour would rise to its apex when dawn broke.

Even the gap seemed familiar, for it had so dominated their thoughts in the past hours. It was difficult to believe the gates had ever been there. Hard to comprehend that it was ever any different. That it had not always been a jagged void with the pathetic remnants of a barricade piled on either side of it.

Only the Dylak tents came as a shock.

They sprawled within the compound like ugly fungoid growths. They were small and flat-topped, each intended to shelter four or five warriors. They were made of untanned animal skins, and they gave forth an odour of decay.

With two exceptions.

Those two tents stood close together, but apart from the others. They were bell-shaped and of the fine Aletta silk. Each would have accommodated all their persons without difficulty.

And it was to one of these that they were taken. In a long crocodile formation, they were pushed through the open flap. And there, surprisingly, their bonds we cut.

They blinked when they were inside. It was almost as bright as day in there. Tall, sheep's-fat torches in silver holders gave vivid illumination.

They stood on rich rugs which entirely concealed the bare ground.

They were confronted by two chairs of carved ivory, padded with lush cushioning. They were occupied by the man and the woman. He was smiling again. She was not. It was he who spoke.

'I have brought you here,' he said smoothly, 'because you, all of you, may be able to help me and thereby preserve your lives. As I said earlier, it is a matter entirely for each one of you. I make the offer only because I have been impressed by the courage with which you attempted to defend this fort.'

He licked his lips, his tongue showing oddly red. And Rex whispered to Pete: 'He's one helluva liar.'

' . . . But first I will make my identity clear, and I will answer any questions which your commanding officer cares to put.'

Subconsciously, it seemed, he drew himself upright. Then he continued: 'I am El Zanal, sheik-paramount of all the Dylaks, and the great-grandson of El Kavah, once Sultan of All Morocco.'

He paused, as though to give the announcement greater impact. And as he did so, Pete's brain began to whirl and to stretch in an effort to recall some half-forgotten knowledge.

It was the mention of the name 'El Kavah' that did it.

Then Pete remembered. El Kavah had been a noted figure in the course of French colonial development during the middle part of the previous century.

In spite of resistance among his own people, he had made and kept a treaty of friendship with France.

And he had taken a French wife . . .

A white woman . . .

Pete looked hard at Tania.

Those white features of hers . . . A throwback? Could that be it? It happened sometimes in mixed marriages. Two or three generations would go by, and all the children would be coloured, or partly so. Then one would be born who appeared to be entirely white.

Outwardly, Pete retained his normal aspect of phlegmatic indifference. Inwardly, he was a seething cauldron. He longed for a chance to speak with Monclaire, who would understand.

But El Zanal was talking again.

He purred on: 'You are doubtless wondering why I and my people have without warning made war on you . . . Why we have left our traditional lands under the Atlas Mountains in order to attack isolated Legion forces.

'So let me first assure you on one point — this is *not* a rebellion against the French in all Morocco. I am not stupid enough to attempt such a thing, for it would fail, just as the attempt by the Bormone people failed.

'But we intend that those parts of Morocco which are by tradition ours shall be returned to us. These are the areas of Nioro and Senegal.

'For years we have attempted to negotiate with the French about this. But they would not even speak with us. For they do not recognize us as an independent people . . . '

His voice shook. A multi-ringed hand made a trembling gesture.

'The French are content to let us remain on sufferance in the barren lands below the mountains. And they will give us access to no other places. We may not use the places where the corn grows and the fresh water flows free . . .

'So, in the years, I have prepared. I have prepared not for war such as you know it, but for a series of isolated attacks upon the French forces. You have experienced only the start of it. Legion columns, Legion forts such as this, will be assailed in all parts of the Sahara. And after we strike, we will vanish. And in the end, the French will lick their wounds and be glad to let us have those lands which are rightfully ours.'

There was a stir of movement. It came from Monclaire. El Zanal regarded him contemptuously.

'You wish to speak, *capitaine*?'

'I do.' Monclaire's incisive tones contrasted with the sibilance of those of the Dylak.

'You have my permission to do so.'

It was an oblique insult, but Monclaire ignored it.

He said, speaking quickly: 'The lands you claim are not yours by tradition or any other right. They are inhabited by independent people under the protection of France. They themselves would be the first to resist any attempt by you to dominate them.'

'You speak foolishly, *capitaine*. The lands were ours in the days of my grandfather.'

'They were — until he voluntarily ceded them by treaty. As he ceded many other possessions which his people could not administer, and to which they had no right. Your grandfather, El Kavah, was a humane and enlightened man. But when he died his policies were abandoned. It seems that he has spawned a family of criminal fools.'

El Zanal's hand went to the hilt of his dagger.

As he half-drew it from its sheath, he was stayed by Tania.

Tania had risen from the ivory chair. Her eyes were staring as though they were green pools of blindness.

Her slender hands shook until they came to rest on her narrow waist.

'*Le capitaine* is slow to learn. Twice in a few hours, he lets his tongue rule his head. Perhaps we can help him. A man's tongue is so easily removed, is it not?'

133

Monclaire ignored her. Never during her venom-laden words did he so much as glance at her. He continued addressing El Zanal as though she had not spoken.

'But, since you have taken the trouble to tell me of your futile ambitions, perhaps you will also answer two other questions?'

El Zanal's hand had left the dagger. Some of the tension had departed from his feline body.

'Perhaps I shall, *capitaine*.'

'Your men have modern repeating rifles. Also grenades with muzzle cups. They are a formidable combination when added to natural treachery. How did you obtain them?'

'It was not difficult, *capitaine*. After the world war, many arms were left stored along the African coast. It was not difficult to arrange for some of them to disappear and be brought to me. I had to pay, of course. But it was well worth it, I think. For now my people do not fight the Legion with muzzle-loading muskets which may explode in the face. They meet them on better than equal terms. Terms which have enabled us to capture a fort, *capitaine*.'

Monclaire nodded.

'*Oui*. I thought that was the explanation. And now, perhaps you will say what it is you want of us? Why have we not been butchered, as our helpless and wounded comrades were butchered?'

El Zanal paused, as though gathering his thoughts. Tania glided back to her chair.

He said: 'It was my first intention to kill you all, then retire until the time was opportune to strike elsewhere. But the knowledge that Colonel Panton, commandant at Dini Sadazi, is on his way here has caused me to change my plans.'

Monclaire looked startled. It was the first time he had shown any such emotion, and El Zanal enjoyed the spectacle.

'You are disturbed at the extent of my knowledge, *capitaine*! But there is nothing surprising about it. Your office files were captured undamaged. The wireless signal from the colonel was there. It made most interesting reading. Most interesting.

'So I thought we could complete our work by planning a reception for the colonel with his three companies and half a battery of horse artillery.'

'When he approaches, we will let him think that the fort is still in your hands. We will make the necessary repairs to the gates. And legionnaires — real legionnaires — will be on the ramparts to greet him. The correct recognition signals will be exchanged. Then the gates will open and he and his men will march into the fort. Need I tell you what will happen after that? My men will descend on them. It will be all over in a few minutes. The legionnaires, taken utterly by surprise and bottled up in the confines of four walls, will not be able to resist. It will be a stroke — a masterstroke — which will force even the government of France to listen to me . . . '

El Zanal spoke with a swift fluency. Thus many of the legionnaires there could only follow the gist of his words. But the gist was enough. A sort of grunting moan escaped from them. It was a simultaneous expression of fear and horror.

Monclaire — even Monclaire — seemed to recoil as though struck by a hard physical blow. And a strange flush appeared under the sickly pallor of his skin.

But he recovered quickly. He tried to bluff.

'It is an ingenious piece of infamy, El Zanal. But it has no chance of success. For one thing, what makes you imagine that my legionnaires would help in such work?'

'A few of them will, *capitaine*. There are more than twenty of your men here. Most, perhaps, will refuse, and it will be amusing to watch them die. But the others . . . there are always others who will betray in order to live . . . in order to escape a terrible death. Those will be my terms — the legionnaires who assist me will be spared. Those who do not . . . '

He broke off with a shrug.

Under his breath, Monclaire uttered a mixture of profanity and prayer.

He knew that what El Zanal said was

true. Utterly true. His legionnaires had already seen something of the Dylak torture methods. So some would submit to El Zanal's terms. It was not a question of courage or cowardice. It went deeper than that. Those who submitted could not be blamed.

Monclaire tried again.

'You have overlooked another fact, El Zanal.'

'I have? Please tell me.'

'While you were attacking the fort, I sent a request to Sadazi for an air strike on your positions. That will take time, but the planes will be over tomorrow.'

El Zanal showed cat-like teeth.

'You are mistaken, *capitaine*.'

'*Ah non!*'

'*Mais oui!* It happens that I have also examined the cypher slips in the wireless room. The system there is perfectly simple. As soon as a message has been transmitted, the operator puts a mark in red pencil on it. It then goes into a special drawer. You wrote a message requesting an air strike, *capitaine*, and telling of our attack upon you. But it was not sent. It was found on the table — unmarked. I persuaded the operator to tell me this. And I have confirmed it against other messages which have been transmitted.'

He was smiling. She was smiling. Their common amusement seemed to give them an even closer affinity. The masculine and the feminine of triumphant evil.

Monclaire fingered the raw whip lashes on his cheek. He touched the great bruise on his forehead. Every legionnaire there sensed the tumult within his mind. And they sensed, too, that he was defeated. There was no card left for him to play.

But they were astounded at his words. Words which seemed to contradict every facet of the man's character.

For Monclaire shrugged his shoulders in a typically Gallic gesture. Then he said: 'Have we your word before the things you hold sacred that if we co-operate with you, our lives will be spared?'

Even El Zanal looked surprised. And, for a moment, suspicious. But the expression of helpless enquiry on Monclaire's face satisfied him.

'Yes — my word before Allah.'

'I would accept that, but it is not enough.'

'You have little choice, *capitaine*. It is a matter of indifference to me whether you personally choose to live or die. As I have said, there will be a few legionnaires here who will co-operate.'

Monclaire shook his head.

'I was not quite thinking of that. I was thinking that if we do as you say, it would not be much use to us if you were to leave us in the desert to die of thirst. Or to be caught and tried as traitors by our own people. Perhaps you would receive more willing assistance if you were to give an additional promise.'

'And that is?'

'To allow each man who helps you a small sum of money — and facilities for getting to the coast. Then, at least, there would be a chance of starting anew and escaping French justice.'

Rex was staring blankly at Monclaire.

'Jeez,' he said in a penetrating whisper. 'That just can't be the captain talking! Who'd have thought that guy'd have turned yellow?'

Monclaire heard. And the flush came back to his face.

But El Zanal was saying: 'I may consider such extra facilities. My decision would largely depend on the quality of help I receive. I will be quite frank — it is most essential that Colonel Panton suspects nothing until he is within the fort. A convincing — er — performance on the ramparts by the legionnaires would be a great help. It would dispose me to reciprocate . . . '

He paused, and added: 'But let me emphasise that there would be no chance of warning the colonel. Kneeling at the back of each legionnaire will be two of my Dylaks — with knives. It is easy to kill a man silently and hold him upright on the ramparts. That would be the only result of any foolishness.

'Oh . . . and there is another matter. Just in case the sudden break in wireless transmission arouses any suspicion at Sadazi, I have instructed the operator to make the necessary repairs. He is doing so now — under guard. I will then cause a suitable explanation to be transmitted, which will allay any fears.'

Tania leaned forward. There was a suggestion of vibrating impatience about her svelte body.

She said: 'Enough! Let us know now which intend to help us, and which will die.'

For the first time during the interview, Monclaire turned towards her. He bowed slightly.

'I will try to persuade all my legionnaires to do as you wish, for I do not see that any useful purpose would be served if some were to refuse. But at the moment I suspect there are a few who do not share my view. I ask for an opportunity to speak to them alone.'

She said: 'And you think you can convince them?'

'*Madame*, I am certain of it. They will see that they have done their duty, and that this is no time for sentimental considerations.'

She touched her lips with the tip of her tongue. It was a characteristically feline gesture. Pete watched her. He found a sinister fascination in her. Somehow, she coalesced the beautiful and the bad. The elegant and the evil. Like an orchid.

Their eyes met. He felt a shiver run through him . . . He recalled the feel of her body. The wicked, sensuous glory of it . . .

They watched each other for several long seconds. It was as though they were alone in that tent. Alone in the whole of Morocco.

Then Tania smiled. There was no tenderness in it. Only sadistic lust.

'And you,' she said, slowly pointing to Pete, 'you, who dared to lay hands on me. Tomorrow you will pay. You will be flogged . . . thirty strokes . . . and I — I, Tania — will myself wield the whip . . . '

8

The Colonel

Briefly, let us digress.

Let us leave Fort Valeau for a few moments and visit a spot some two hundred and fifty kilometres west.

Colonel Panton was in high spirits towards the end of the first day. He turned in the saddle of his white charger and surveyed the long column of men behind him. Three hundred and sixty marching men. Plus six horse-drawn field guns with their crews.

Such a force had seldom been seen in the desert since the distant days of the Bormone wars. With such a force at his command, plus his own innate ability, the colonel had no doubt that the Dylak trouble would be quickly settled.

In five days they would reach Valeau.

There, he would rest his men for twenty-four hours. Then the hunt for the

Dylaks would commence. It would depend upon the latest information, of course, but the colonel visualised it as a wide sweep of the desert towards the foothills of the Atlas Mountains. As they approached the natural habitat of the Dylaks, then the Dylaks themselves would be increasingly likely to appear. For they would feel that their homes were threatened.

The colonel could see it all.

The decisive battle.

His own brilliantly conceived tactical measures.

The rout of the Dylaks.

The immediate execution of their leaders.

Perhaps, if the circumstances were propitious, he himself would lead the final charge. But even the colonel's imagination tarried at that prospect. He would have to consider whether he was justified in endangering his own valuable life. Not, of course, that it was a matter of personal concern. *Non!* It was purely a matter of his duty to France.

Then Colonel Panton returned to his

dream of the previous day. The dream in which he reported his success to the general. Halfway through it, he decided to halt the column and bivouac for the night.

The colonel felt an urgent need for privacy. He wanted to be alone in the confines of his tent. There he could give way to his thespian impulses. There he could enact again that dramatic scene in which he saluted and said firmly: '*Mon general*, I have formally to report that the Dylaks have been traced and destroyed . . . '

9

Tania

They did not return to the wireless room in Fort Valeau. Instead, Monclaire and his legionnaires were escorted to the main mess room — the place of the surrender. There, they were given water and biscuits from the fort's stores. And then the two guards withdrew to beyond the doors.

There was a harsh atmosphere among that handful of men. The place was heavy with suspicion and disgust.

Monclaire was the centre of it.

They sat on the remaining floorboards and breathed air which still smelled of cordite. They fingered empty cartridge cases which lay around. And they watched Monclaire. The worst and the best of human emotions were being demonstrated among the legionnaires just then.

The worst came from those who agreed

with what Monclaire had said in the tent. Who were glad of a chance of preserving their lives, even at the cost of luring their comrades to massacre. It was those who eyed Monclaire covertly. For they did not wish to show their satisfaction openly. And they were trying to gauge the feelings of the others.

The best came from those who would not trade their lives under such terms. Those who knew deep within themselves that death in any foul form was a better way.

Rex was one of these.

So was Pete.

And Gina — the lieutenant who in the last few hours had found himself.

And Diepel . . .

Monclaire was standing by one of the shattered windows, looking out over the compound at the Dylak guards. The moon was full on his torn and wounded face, giving it a yellow and wan aspect. Suddenly he turned towards the legionnaires. He spoke softly, in the manner of a man who must not be overheard.

He said: 'Many of you hate me for what

I said to El Zanal.'

There was an uncomfortable shuffle. He smiled faintly.

'I'm glad,' he said. 'I never knew that I would live to enjoy the contempt of my men — but it has happened.

'Now, you must listen to me. Listen carefully, *mes legionnaires*. It is essential that you understand . . . '

He groped in the breast pocket of his blood-stained tunic, found his case and took a cigarette from it. When he was smoking:

'In war, when the enemy holds every advantage, only one course is possible. That course is to delay. To use every device to gain time. That is our position now . . . '

The atmosphere of suspicion was fading. The legionnaires listened as they had seldom before listened to an officer.

'No purpose would have been served by openly defying that monster El Zanal. If I had done so, what would have happened? Only the bravest and best would have died. And the weakest would have been left to do his will — to carry out the betrayal.

'Is it not better, therefore, that we meet duplicity with duplicity? That we use any means to remain together? That we do our best to convince El Zanal that we'll buy our lives on his foul terms? For remember, there are yet five days before the column is due here. In that time we may, between us, conceive of some way of warning them.'

Rex stood up. Monclaire glanced towards him and waited for him to speak.

'That makes sense to me, Captain. And I guess you put on a helluva good bluff. But I can't figure out how we can warn the column. We're prisoners in here, and there doesn't seem much chance of getting out. But suppose one of us does get out? He'd only die in the desert.'

Monclaire nodded. Then Rex went on: 'And I don't see there's much chance of warning them when they arrive outside the fort gates. We heard what that punk said — any legionnaire who attempted to bawl out would be quietly knifed and held upright like nothing had happened. And

150

there's something else that makes it worse. These columns nearly always arrive towards nightfall. That's when the last one was due. In full daylight, they might notice something and get suspicious. But not at night.'

'So you think it is hopeless, *mon legionnaire?*'

'Not hopeless, Captain, but goddamned difficult. The Dylaks look like they hold all the aces, plus a few extra cards from another pack. It looks like we've gotta do a lot of hard thinking.'

Monclaire carefully nipped out his half-smoked cigarette and replaced it in his case. It was his last.

'As you say, *legionnaire*, a lot of hard thinking. For we are in the hands of a fanatic — a political fanatic. He cannot realise that his plans will have only one result — a terrible retribution on his people. He is bent only on slaughter. And he has genius — make no mistake about that. There was genius in the plan which took this fort. That, plus treachery. And there is terrible genius in the plan to lure Colonel Panton's column here . . . '

He pushed his hands into his leather tunic belt and advanced towards the legionnaires. His face had changed. It had become utterly hard. Utterly unrelenting.

He seemed to embrace each one of them in his glittering eyes.

He said: 'A way must be found. A way will be found. But let this be understood. If any legionnaire repeats a word of what has been said here, then I will kill him. Nothing will save him. The whole race of Dylaks will be unable to protect him. I, Monclaire, will kill him myself . . . '

★   ★   ★

The night.

The velvet blackness over the wastelands.

Most of those legionnaires slept — after a fashion. They sprawled over the bare floor without blankets to shield them from the cold. Some mumbled in their sleep. Thick words recalled half-forgotten places and people. Some swore, continuously and instinctively. One very young legionnaire sobbed: the quiet sobbing of nerves that have been stretched beyond breaking point.

One man scarcely slept at all. He lay, head cushioned on his arms, staring at an invisible ceiling.

It was Pete.

And in his mind's eye, Pete saw Tania. The lovely witch who had made the fantastic threat to flog him.

* * *

It was no idle threat.

The sun was climbing the eastern sky when the legionnaires were escorted (with the aid of kicks) into the open compound. There, they were formed into a single line, facing the two great tents.

Between those tents, a nine-foot wood stake had been driven deep into the ground. A thick iron ring was secured into the top of it.

Dylaks had assembled in hundreds. Save for the small space around the stake, they entirely filled the west side of the compound. Others had climbed onto the ramparts to have a better view. There was an atmosphere of salacious expectation. Not much noise. Only a faint surge of Arabic talk.

Rex and Monclaire were standing on either side of Pete. Rex glanced at him, tried to grin, and said: 'Bud, it looks like that bitch wasn't joking any.'

And Monclaire touched Pete's arm.

'I'll try to stop this barbarism,' he said. '*Dieu* . . . to flog a man is one thing! But for a woman to do it . . . '

Pete shook his head. If he felt any emotion, it did not reveal itself in his smooth, slightly cynical voice.

'Nothing can be done, so it's better not to try. Y'know, I was always one for pleasing the ladies. If this amuses this particular lady, who are we to stand in her way?'

Rex grunted. There were times when Pete's Englishness was beyond his understanding.

It was at that moment that Tania and El Zanal appeared out of their tents.

They stood under the awning for a few moments, looking at the legionnaires. Brown brother and white sister. Different in colour. But the bonds of evil which bound them were forged in the womb.

And as they stood, he was greeted by the sweeping cry, 'Zanal!'

There was something almost courtly in the way he acknowledged them. His left foot went back a few inches and he gave a slow, shallow bow. In most people, such a gesture would have been ridiculous. In El Zanal, it epitomised regal dignity. Yet it was not typical of the Dylaks.

At first, Pete was puzzled by it. He found it impossible to reconcile the gesture with the man. Then he remembered. It was not only Tania who had white blood in her. He, her brother, also carried the blood of France in his veins.

Then he looked at Tania.

She was wearing no headdress, and her raven hair flowed to her silk-robed shoulders. She wore little beneath that robe, for each slight movement of her body was reflected in the shimmering material.

And there was an exquisite hell in her green eyes. In the sunlight, the pupils had contracted to fine points. They were still pools of ill-omen. Pete looked into them and was held by them. But she did not return his stare. Instead, she made a brief gesture to the Dylak guards.

Four of them grabbed Pete and pulled him out of the file. They dragged him to Tania, not stopping until they were within a foot of her.

Even then, she did not look directly at Pete. She seemed to look through and beyond him.

And she said: 'You are about to be humbled, Legionnaire. You are about to plead and cry for mercy. But you will receive none.'

Her words were like a claw on velvet. The tones — soft, lovely. The meaning of them — unnaturally repulsive.

She had spoken in French. Pete chose to answer in English.

'I never plead,' he said, 'for things that I cannot possibly receive.'

She understood. That was obvious by the way her big eyes suddenly became just a trifle smaller and her body tensed.

But she did not answer. Instead, she made another gesture. Pete was dragged towards the stake.

They dragged off his tunic, baring his brown, muscular body. Then they lashed his wrists together and secured them with a loose thong to the iron ring, so that he stood helpless with his arms stretched high above his head. There was a babble of excited anticipation from the Dylaks. It died quickly away when the whip was handed to Tania.

It was a vastly different instrument to the riding whip.

The stock was of bound ebony. The plaiting of that leather continued into the lash itself. The tip was divided into four short sections, each bearing six quarter-inch knots. The whole length was well over twelve feet. It was a whip which could kill with ease.

She nursed it in her hands. She caressed it. Then, with a deft flick of her strong wrist, she sent the lash snaking into the air. The crack was as loud as that of a Lebel. But it contained a hollow horror that never came from a Lebel.

The sound seemed to satisfy her. She

was smiling as she glided towards the stake.

She stood facing Pete's bare back, and within reach of it. She studied it speculatively. And she was still smiling as she moved away and to one side.

Carefully, she paced her distance. She assessed it so that the tips of the thongs would wrap themselves round Pete's waist.

The last remnants of noise had vanished from the compound. The place was a vast coalescence of intent faces. Callously intent Dylak faces. Sensitively intent Legion ones.

She jerked back the lash, then, with a smooth bodily movement which was like that of a dancer, she reversed its progress. It travelled faster than the eye could detect. It only became visible again when the ends of it were coiled round Pete's body.

The impact made little sound. No more than a faint slap. But Pete's back arched unnaturally and a coughing groan came from deep in his throat.

She jerked the lash free.

Where there had been firm, strong flesh there were now vivid channels of red hell, stretching from rib to rib.

The long leather lash repeated its course. It cut again into the same places.

This time Pete made no sound. But, convulsively, he flung his feet in the air, and for a second was supported only by his wrists.

Tania paused. Paused to laugh. It was a gentle, penetrating sound. And an utterly happy one. Like the playing of the morning breeze. Or the purr of a cat over its kill.

And she said: 'Go on — do a jig, my English friend! Do a jig for Tania! But perhaps you are wanting more encouragement, more inspiration . . .'

She raised the whip.

Rex turned to Monclaire. His face looked as if it had been immersed in a bath of grease.

'We've gotta stop it. We can't stand here and let that hellcat . . .'

But Monclaire was not listening. He was watching as though hypnotised. Rex pulled feverishly at his sleeve. Then

Monclaire came out of his seeming trance.

'There is nothing we can do,' he said dully. 'Nothing. But he may not suffer too much. Nature itself has a way of protecting its own. You will see.'

Rex's mind swirled like that of a man in a fever. *Nothing we can do. Nothing.* Just got to stand there and watch a man being welted to ribbons by a fiend . . .

He knew Monclaire was right. They could attempt to rush to Pete's aid. But they'd be overpowered before they got anywhere near him. And maybe the diversion would only make it worse for Pete. If it was possible for it to be any worse . . .

And Pete . . .

Pete counted the strokes. Each one bit into his mind as well as his body. After the seventh stroke, he knew that his senses were going. He could no longer see. Only a maze of red was before his eyes.

And the agony seemed to be fading. As though some rich balm were being applied. He had a hazy idea he was back in England . . . back in the mess and enjoying that pre-lunch party . . . back in his car and running into that old gentleman . . . back in the court when the judge pronounced sentence . . .

He was unconscious when the lash descended for the eighth time. He hung, and spun slightly by his wrists from the stake.

★   ★   ★

She crossed over to him and waited. The whip was still in her hands, and the blood-tinted thongs trailed in the sand.

Her face was close to his when at last his eyes flickered open. Deliberately, she waited until his mind had cleared. Until he had stifled the moans which rose in his throat.

Then she said: 'There are still twenty-two strokes left. I have the strength to deliver them. Have you the strength to survive them? I think not.'

Pete did not answer. He did not accept the invitation of her pause.

She added: 'You may spare your life, my friend. You may do it by descending to your knees at my feet before my people, and asking that I spare you . . .'

She waited. Still he did not answer. The only sound was the deep panting of his breath.

'Come — you are fortunate. I, Tania, do not usually make terms. Will you do this — or do you prefer to die under the lash?'

It was then that Pete answered. His voice came as a faint croak, so that only she heard it. And somehow he contrived to force his dust-covered face into a parody of that cynical smile.

He said: 'I — I think you have inherited your beauty from France . . . but your mind . . . your mind is the gift of the devil . . . ' Then his jaw fell slack. And again he succumbed gladly to the relief of unconsciousness.

El Zanal came up to her. He looked at her then at the inert, tortured figure.

'Are you continuing with the lash?' he asked. 'Or shall I give the task to a warrior?'

He did not notice that her lips were trembling.

She said: 'I have seen enough. I am satisfied. Let him go.'

10

The Visit

The office which had been Monclaire's was scarcely recognisable as such. Five legionnaires had fought and died in there. The red-spattered walls, the bullet-chipped stonework, were tokens of their resistance. And there was no furniture. That had gone the way of all other movable items. Except for the desk. In the urgency of the moment, there had not been time to get this, an awkward piece, out of the narrow door.

It was this desk which had proved so invaluable to El Zanal. In it, he had found the wireless signals. And now, he had found a detailed scale map of the fort itself.

He stood under the shattered window of the room and studied that map. And as he did so, he decided that it would make his plans vastly easier. He could see now at a glance (without having to make a detailed survey) how he could best conceal and dispose his men until the gates were safely closed behind the last of Colonel Panton's column.

Some, he would place inside the buildings. These corridors here, those corridors there, would provide easy exits when the signal was given to attack.

But most of his warriors could safely wait in the open — on the east side. They would be hidden from the approaching Legion column by the compound buildings themselves. And when the moment came, they could stream round from either side.

The horses had been a problem.

There were more than a thousand of the animals. They could not, as now, be left tethered in the compound when the column arrived. But the plan gave the answer. Here, below ground, was the magazine. If the scale were right, it would accommodate nearly half of them.

The others would have to be driven off

shortly before the column was due. There was every prospect of recapturing the majority.

Swiftly, El Zanal's agile mind darted from problem to problem, conceiving the answers to each.

But always he returned to the moment when the column would pause outside the fort. This was the truly vital time. There must be no hitch — no possibility of a hitch. That was why he was reluctantly compelled to use legionnaires on the ramparts. Dylaks in Legion uniforms would not do. Their features might not be detected, but their demeanour would almost certainly arouse suspicion. No power on earth, El Zanal admitted to himself, would give a Dylak warrior the military bearing of a legionnaire. And they would be unable to ask and answer the routine recognition questions. So the legionnaires had to be used.

They amused him, that motley handful of beaten men.

A little while ago, Captain Monclaire had told him that all of them would co-operate — in exchange for their lives and a safe passage to the coast. The captain had been almost servile.

And he, El Zanal, had undertaken to respect their lives. On the matter of the safe passage, he refused to commit himself. That had made his promise appear the more convincing. And they might as well be convinced, those legionnaires. For they would all die when they had served their purpose.

El Zanal pushed the plan under his robes and left the office. On the way to his tent he turned his mind to the more distant future. To the time when the massacre was over. He felt confident that the French — already troubled with revolt in another colony — would be glad to treat with him. Glad to recognise the independence of his people and their right to the territories of Nioro and Senegal.

Thenceforward, the possibilities were without limit. For everywhere, it seemed, the power of the western races was declining. He — a Dylak with the blood of France within him — could be in the forefront of a renaissance in North Africa . . .

In the wireless room . . .

The Polish legionnaire had completed the repairs to his equipment. It had been a difficult task, and he was rather proud of the way he had accomplished it.

But he was not proud now, as he sat beside his Morse key and tapped out a message. He had been told that ghastly things would be done to him if it were found that the message had not been transmitted exactly as prescribed. That might not have intimidated him. He might have taken a chance if it had been only a matter of his own skin. But he had also been told that all the other legionnaires would immediately be slaughtered.

So, in a series of short and long buzzes, the Polish legionnaire tapped a signal:

To Commandant's Secretary, Dini Sadazi. From Commanding Officer, Fort Valeau. — Regret interruption in transmission at 18.00 hours yesterday. Due to technical fault.

168

Was about to enquire whether my garrison will now come under direct command of Colonel Panton.

The reply was received within ten minutes. It was terse. It said:

To Commanding Officer. Fort Valeau. From Commandant's Secretary, Dini Sadazi. — Obviously.

And there was some heavy head-shaking among the staff officers at Sadazi at that moment. It appeared that Monclaire was losing his grip! Such ignorance of such a simple matter of routine! It was extraordinary!

★ ★ ★

In Tania's tent . . .

She had reached a decision. It had not taken long, for it was inevitable in a creature of her strange and dark temperament.

She opened the flap and said to one of her personal guards: 'The man that was flogged . . . has he yet recovered?'

The guard did not know. But he would enquire.

Tania nodded. And she said: 'If he is, bring him to me . . . '

They had made Pete as comfortable as they could. Every legionnaire had taken off his tunic and laid it on the floor. Together, they formed an improvised mattress. He lay on it — on his stomach.

A full twenty-four hours had passed since the lash had cut into his back. But the agony had not abated. It had merely changed its form. It was no longer a series of searing brands on the surface of the skin. Now it was a massive contraction of every muscle of his body. Like an all-embracing cramp.

The medical officer had not been able to help much. He was still in a dazed state after the slaughter of the wounded in his sick bay. And he was refused permission to draw on the medical supplies. So he had fumbled over the tortured skin for a while, until Pete swore at him. Then, still dazed, he had gone away.

Rex had offered greater comfort. Rex

had squatted down in front of him, and held his hand during the long hell of the night. And he had lit cigarettes for him and put them in his mouth.

Monclaire had helped, too. Monclaire had spoken to him of Paris. Of places that were familiar to both of them. At first, Pete had not wanted to hear him. But gradually, he found himself listening. And there were times when he almost forgot his pain. It was sometime in the early morning, when he felt a little delirious, that Pete told Monclaire that he had served in the British Army. He told of the accident . . . Monclaire's face softened. And when it was all over he said: 'We have something special in common, *mon lieutenant.*'

Those trite words made Pete feel better.

It was midday when the Dylak guard came in. He stood over Pete. Then, with obvious reluctance, he bent down and attempted to pull him to his feet.

Pete had been dozing. He gave out a groan.

At the same moment, Rex acted. He took a few fast paces up to the Dylak, poised himself, then drove his right fist into the Arab's ribs.

It was not a punch which would have been approved in any prize ring. It was too near the kidneys. But Rex was in no mood to concern himself with niceties. It served its purpose. The Dylak grunted, let go his grasp on Pete, then slumped to the floor.

In that moment Rex felt his spirits surge. He had done something to help cancel out the feeling of impotence — even if it was only to slug a single Dylak!

But it was a brief sensation of triumph.

Even as he stood exulting, four other guards, attracted by the noise, came rushing in. One of them brought the hilt of his sabre down on Rex's skull. He was unconscious before he started to fall.

Then the guards jerked Pete to his feet. And they forced him to walk out of the building and to Tania's tent.

★   ★   ★

A sea of treacle. It rolled slowly, stickily, within Pete's head. It cloyed each thinking particle of his mind. He was only vaguely aware that the guards had gone. And that he was alone with Tania.

He knew that somehow he was staying on his feet. But he was swaying. He must be swaying. For the silken walls were moving like a pendulum.

Something was put into his hand. Something cool and slender. Reluctantly, it came into focus. It was a quartz goblet. Half-filled with a deep red liquid. A voice said: 'Drink it . . . I want to talk with you . . . drink it . . . it will help . . . '

It was her voice. The sweetly satanic voice.

He wanted to throw the goblet into her face. Wanted to see the liquid splash and sting those green eyes. And stain the delicate loveliness of her features.

But she was repeating those words. There was compulsion in them.

' . . . *I want to talk with you . . . drink it . . .* '

He got the goblet to his lips. The stuff burned his throat. Then it lit fires in his stomach. But, quite suddenly, his brain began to clear. The tent became steady.

He saw her clearly. She was standing within a foot of him. Looking straight at him. Looking into him. Tall, slim, in scarlet robes. Like a high priestess of sin.

Pete said, very faintly: 'What do you want with me? Have you not amused yourself enough?'

At first she did not answer. She gestured to a pile of rich cushions.

'Sit there. You're not strong enough to stand.'

He was glad to obey. And as he did so he became aware of the raw nudity of the upper part of his body. He could not resist it. He said: 'I'm not properly dressed for visiting a lady.'

She smiled. That cat-like smile.

'You are not to blame for that, Legionnaire. But you are fortunate. I have killed men with the lash. I could have killed you. Do you know why I did not?'

She waited for an answer. There was none. So she continued: 'I think there were two reasons. One of them was because you showed courage. But the other one was more important. You talked to me of France. Do you remember? Even as you writhed in agony, you said . . . '

Pete interrupted.

' . . . I said that you inherited your beauty from France. But your mind was the gift of the devil.'

'You did. Now, tell me — why did you link me with France?'

'You are white.'

'A mere chance. Obviously my skin is a throwback from one of my forebears. But a white skin could come from any of many races. What makes you so certain that it is French blood that flows within me? Why not Spanish, or Italian, or even English?'

She was leaning over him, body arched. And there was an urgency about her.

Pete said: 'It happens that I have read the history of El Kavah and his marriage to Maria D'Anton, the daughter of a marshal of France. It is an unusual story. A story that stays in the mind. El Kavah was a great man. She was an exceptional woman. I can congratulate you and your brother upon your ancestry, madame, but not upon your achievements.'

She sucked in a deep breath. Her hand

went to her breast. For the first time, Pete noticed a gold locket there. It was heart-shaped, small and exquisitely worked. Obviously a piece of European craftsmanship. Her fingers played with it.

She ignored the insult and said gently: 'I did not know that legionnaires were so well acquainted with such matters. The captain — what is his name . . . ?'

'Monclaire.'

'*Ah, oui*, Monclaire. I would have expected him to know this. And I would have expected him also to guess at the reason for the colour of my skin. But you . . . you puzzle me.'

'Many kinds of people find their way into the Legion, madame. It is an army of odd characters.'

'Apparently.' She watched him carefully, then added: 'You are right, of course. I and my brother are descended from Maria D'Anton. But we are not proud of the fact! Not proud . . . you understand! We are Dylaks. Our people are Dylaks. And the French are our enemies . . .

She took her hand from the locket and

placed it against her cheek.

'This white flesh of mine is a curse! It is an eternal shame! I can atone for it only by unrelenting hate against France and all who serve France . . . '

Her voice trailed away in a strangled choke.

Pete looked at her in astonishment. She was no longer the complete master of herself. It was as though a mask was slipping away. And he felt embarrassed.

The stimulation of the wine was wearing off, too. He felt the swirling sickness returning. And he was fully aware of the pains in all his muscles.

He wanted to get out. Out of the fetid luxury of the tent. Back to the others. To Rex, and Monclaire, and Diepel. People he could understand . . .

He tried to get to his feet.

But the tent began to sway again. Just as it had done when he first came in. Like a pendulum. And the sea of treacle surged again in his head.

He knew he would not be able to stand. He could not leave this place without help. But he did not want to stay.

For some reason he was afraid to stay . . .

Two hands were pressing against the front of his shoulders. They were running down the sides of his torn body. Cool, gentle hands. They seemed to draw out the pain.

He heard her speak, as though from a long way off. Yet there was no mistaking her words.

She said: '*Dieu* . . . did I do this . . . ?'

And then she almost lifted him onto his stomach. And he lay among the cushions while she rubbed balm into his wounds. It brought quick relief.

Then she refilled the quartz goblet. But this time she held it to his lips.

She was kneeling before him and slightly over him. Pete felt the warm glow of her body — as he had felt it before. It was the sort of body that etched itself like acid into the pockets of the mind. Rich and sensual.

There was a perfume. The sort of perfume that seems to be a natural and glorious part of a woman, rather than a mere application.

Pete did not intend to stretch out his

hand to her. It simply happened — happened without any prior decision on his part. The tips of his fingers were against her cheek. She did not draw away. Her green eyes were heavy as they looked into his.

Then he folded her in his arms.

11

Preparation

Night was falling when Pete rejoined the others. There was no guard with him. Rex regarded him curiously.

'Say, what gives? That back of yours . . . it looks a helluva lot better. You seem like a stronger man. We've all been thinking that witch was going to take you apart again.'

Pete looked round carefully. The other legionnaires were watching him. But they were out of hearing if he kept his voice down. He wanted desperately to confide in Rex. But instinct prompted him not to do so.

He said, simply: 'The pain's wearing off.'

There was a heavy silence. Rex eyed him with careful calculation.

Then he said: 'You didn't even have a Dylak to keep you company when you came in here. It looks like you have suddenly become an important guy around this joint.'

There was an inference in the statement. Concealed, but there just the same. Pete's cheeks were flushed when he answered.

'I suppose a guard is superfluous. There's no chance of getting out of here.'

'Ain't there?'

'Well, you can see for yourself, can't you?'

Unconsciously, both had raised their voices. And they were almost glaring at each other.

Then Rex relaxed. He gave a grin and said, less loudly: 'Look, bud, you've been out of here for a long time. Something's been happening. We're all in this together, so maybe you'd better let us know about it.'

The words hit Pete like a kick. His mind reeled. And, through the confusion, one question kept repeating itself. *How can I let them know? How can I?* How could he explain that Tania had a hypnotic fascination for him? That he had really been aware of it from the moment he first saw her on horseback immediately after the surrender ... that it had survived even the humiliation and the agony of the lash? If he told them, they would think him crazy. And his innate reserve rebelled against discussing such things.

So Pete said, coldly: 'Nothing had happened that would interest you.'

Rex had been squatting on some of the piled-up tunics. He rose suddenly. There was something akin to fury in his face.

'So it wouldn't interest us, huh! We know where you've been, bud. One of the Dylaks told us. We've been worrying about you. We've been thinking that maybe you'd be brought back here in a lot of separate pieces. But you don't. You look a different guy, all right. But not worse. You look one hundred per cent better. And in case you've forgotten, let me remind you that your breath stinks of ripe wine and you're using a nice line in perfume! Come on. We're entitled to know. Tell us what's been happening!'

Pete did not answer. He shrugged his

bare shoulders. Monclaire had been listening curiously. He came over.

He said to Rex: 'That's enough, Legionnaire. I will ask any questions — if questions are necessary.'

His informality of the past few days had gone. It was a terse order from an officer. Rex opened his mouth to protest. Then, probably because he shared the general respect for Monclaire, he turned away silently.

Monclaire's face relaxed into a half-smile as he looked down at Pete. He rubbed the bristles on his chin.

'*Mon legionnaire*, I think it would be better if you were to make a report to me. You must have seen many things while you were out of here, and any scraps of information may be important to us. But there is no hurry. No doubt you are still in pain and tired. We'll discuss it tomorrow.'

He was about to move to his corner of the room. Pete called him back.

'*Capitaine*.'

'*Oui*.'

'You might as well know that there's no

report I can possibly make. None at all.'

Monclaire was by no means an old man. He was at the rich stage of life which combines the spring of youth with the experience of maturity. But at that moment the lines of sheer senility etched themselves into his face.

Pete watched it happening. The spectacle hurt him. It was like betraying a trust.

Monclaire said: 'You are sure of that, *mon legionnaire*?'

'I'm sure, *capitaine*.'

And then Monclaire walked away, squaring his slim shoulders.

There was a rumble of sullen talk among the legionnaires.

Rex came back to Pete.

'Goddam it,' Rex said feverishly. 'Can't you understand? Don't you know what we're all thinking?'

'Well — what *are* you thinking?'

Rex's tough, good-natured face was twitching. He hesitated.

A perverse madness got into Pete. He added, shouting: 'Go on — tell me! Or perhaps you haven't the guts!'

Rex's face went white. The whiteness of a threatening cloud. He grated out each word.

'Okay, if that's the way you want it . . . we're thinking that maybe you've done a deal with the Dylaks. A genuine deal. We're thinking that maybe you're gonna . . . '

He did not finish the sentence. Pete jerked suddenly up from his sitting position. And as he did so, his right fist flashed across the angle of Rex's jaw.

It was a nicely timed punch. But there was no steam behind it. Rex's head jerked back fractionally under the impact. But that was all. He bunched his own big fists. Then he thrust them deep into his tunic pockets.

'I could break you in half for that, Limey,' he said. 'But I guess you're in no condition for fighting. You've taken enough punishment. So long, pal . . . it's been nice knowing you.'

And he moved away from him.

They all moved away from him.

* * *

It was on the following morning that they were set to work. Serious work.

The gates were the main task. It was not a question of repair. The old ones were beyond that. It was a matter of making new ones.

It was fortunate for El Zanal that the equipment of Fort Valeau included large quantities of timber. This had originally been intended for the construction of outbuildings, including stables. But it suited the new purpose admirably.

A dozen legionnaires sweated through the day carrying great beams into the compound and hammering them into a shape.

None of them were carpenters. And as the hours dragged past, it became obvious that the new gates would be little more than an inexact parody of the old. But that did not worry the Dylaks much. As long as they looked like the original gates, they would serve their purpose.

The others had a lighter task.

They cleaned up the more obvious damage in the compound. They collected glass from the store room and replaced the broken panes.

Rex was given the tough work. So was Diepel. So was Monclaire — for no distinction was made in rank. And Gina. Pete, too.

But in Pete's case the work on the gates lasted no more than an hour.

Then an order was received by the Dylak guards. One of them came over to Pete. He was almost deferential as he pointed towards Tania's tent.

Every legionnaire watched as Pete walked away. Watched silently. The sort of pregnant silence that comes when a length of elastic is being stretched too far.

★   ★   ★

That afternoon — with three days to go before the column was due — the Dylaks started a system of rehearsals. Under the supervision of El Zanal, they grouped in the compound buildings, and at a signal came rushing out into the open. This was repeated several times while the number of warriors allotted to each door was adjusted, so as to gain the maximum speed of attack.

When El Zanal was satisfied, he turned his attention to the main body — which would be grouped behind the buildings. These assembled exactly as they would when the column came. They pressed four deep along the entire length of the east walls.

Then El Zanal, accompanied by three pashas, rode out of the west side of the fort. They did not turn back until they had covered more than three miles. And they took the return ride slowly, at no more speed than at which men would march.

When he was back in the fort, the legionnaires heard El Zanal say: 'My warriors were quite invisible. There is no chance of the column seeing them — none.'

★　★　★

Colonel Panton . . .

He, with three days' march still ahead, was becoming steadily less happy. There were dark moments when he doubted his wisdom in personally leading this expedition. It was not that he had the slightest doubt about his capacity to do so. It was simply that he wondered whether, because of his high sense of duty, he was not overtaxing his strength.

After all, the colonel reflected, he was no longer a young man. And this constant movement, this infernal heat, was having a discomforting effect.

It was true that he shared with his staff major and two other senior officers the privilege of horseback. It was difficult to regard that as a compensation. In fact as Colonel Panton rubbed a surreptitious palm over his tender rear quarters, he decided that it might have been better to have marched on foot.

It had crossed his mind that he might depute his immediate command to the major, and return himself to Sadazi after giving detailed operational orders.

Reluctantly, he had dismissed the idea.

Even Colonel Panton realised that his return under such conditions would bear the stamp of the ridiculous Not that anyone would dare say anything, of course He would know how to deal with them if they did. But he would be aware of slighting remarks in dark corners. Such remarks would certainly be made. And, as a result, he would risk losing that high esteem with which he confidently believed his officers and men regarded him.

He was shuffling in the saddle and brooding thus when the staff major (who had been at the rear of the column) rode up. 'I've been checking our position, *mon colonel*. We're making good progress. We should arrive at Valeau according to the estimate — about one hour after nightfall.'

Panton fixed a pair of paunchy eyes on him.

'Is that all you wish to tell me?'

'*Oui, mon colonel*.'

'*Mon Dieu!* Do you think I wish to be concerned with routine nonsense such as that?'

'I — I thought you would be interested in it as a progress confirmation.'

Panton snorted.

'I'm not! You are simply telling me that an estimate is proving correct. I expect them to prove correct. I am only interested when they are in error. I am astounded, Major, at the way in which you burden me with trivialities. You are not being helpful. When this expedition is over I shall have to consider making a report . . . '

The major's face was black with suppressed fury as he rode back to the rear of the column. There he said to a very young lieutenant: 'I forgot to give a message to the colonel. Tell him that our progress is good. Say we should arrive at Valeau soon after darkness three days from now. Don't say that I sent you. Let him think the report is your own idea. He likes initiative in junior officers . . . '

And — human nature being what it is — the staff major felt vastly better as he watched the wretched subaltern start a long trot towards the front of the column.

12

Proposal

Tania said: 'You have not come to me just because I sent for you. You are here because you want to be here.'

She held Pete's hands in her own. Held them tightly, fiercely. And she drew him towards her as they stood together in the centre of the tent.

There was a hoarse, strangled note in his answer. 'Yes, I wanted to come.'

'I knew it. It is two days since we were last alone. Has it seemed very much more . . . has it?'

It was more of a challenge than a question. Pete tried to form words. But he dared not trust his power to do so. Her presence — the fury and the raw passion of it — seemed to atrophy the mind.

After a few moments she drew away from him. She poured wine into two goblets and gave him one.

And she asked: 'Tell me . . . do you think me a fiend? Do you still think I have the mind of the devil?' There was a taunting undertone in the words. Now — now that her body was no longer pressed to his — Pete found he could answer her.

'I do. I think that you are really two people, Tania. Part of you is devil. That is the part you have cultivated.'

'And the other?'

His lips quivered in the merest suggestion of a smile.

'The other is the opposite of devil, Tania. Angel, if you like. But only I have seen that.'

She was serious.

'Yes — only you. And you will never again see the other part of me. For you, my Pete, and only for you, I am a woman.'

She held the glass to her lips. Pete watched the faint tremor of her slender white throat as she swallowed the wine.

And he felt a new and insane desire. He thought: 'I could close my hands round that throat. She would suspect nothing until I pressed with my thumbs. It would be over in a few seconds. Then I would be free — free from her . . . '

But he knew he could never do it. He was held by her. Utterly. Just as he knew she was held by him. It was wrong. It was a contemptible liaison without a future. It had made him an outcast among his friends. But it was inevitable, unalterable, like the stars in their orbits.

He glanced towards the slight aperture over the tent flap. Through it, he saw a thin patch of night sky.

'I must go back, Tania. I've been here too long. El Zanal — your brother — may get to know. It would not matter much to me. I rather think I'm going to die soon anyway. But you . . . ?'

She put down the goblet. She said slowly: 'My brother knows.'

'You — you mean you've told him?'

'I have. And please don't look so startled, Pete! There is nothing to fear for me. He would not dare harm me. And he will never harm you. Never. Not if you are sensible . . . '

Pete took a pace towards her, but she moved away

'No, don't touch me now. I want you to listen to me. I want you to agree with me. You must — you must!'

She had changed again. She almost spat out the last few words. Her body had that feline arch. Poised like a beautiful cat. Pete's arms dropped to his sides.

'Go on,' he said. He had a feeling of helplessness.

'We can always be together — always. Do you understand that? To the end of our time we need never part. I have told my brother that this must be so. Oh, he did not like it! But no one, not even him, stands in the way of Tania! But I cannot make you do this. You must want to do so. You must want to be with me, just as I want to be with you. And you must forget your old loyalties, my Pete. You must have only one loyalty — to me.'

Pete made an impatient gesture. Then he fingered his stained and torn tunic, which he had been able to put on again for the first time that day.

'Tania . . . '

'Yes.'

'I — I couldn't. Don't you understand?

I want you, Tania. I must love you in a way no man has ever loved a woman. But what you ask is impossible. It would never work. No man could betray himself and others that way. And there is a difference between us. There is a huge gulf between our ways of living . . . don't you see . . . ?'

His voice trailed away and ended in a choke of pure misery.

Then he saw the change that had come over Tania.

It almost frightened him.

It was concentrated, all of it, in her eyes and her mouth.

Her eyes . . . they became evil places of green fire. Her mouth . . . it was pulled harshly back, showing teeth that were small, pointed and animal.

Suddenly she was no longer beautiful. She was a distortion of herself. That sibilant hiss was back in her voice.

'It *is* possible and it *will* be so!'

'But I tell you, Tania . . . '

'Quiet! Listen to me! Listen as you have never listened before! I said just now that I could not make you do this. I said it because I wanted you to feel free and glad when you accepted me. But I can make you. I *can* . . .

'And I shall. I shall because I want you even more than you want me. Whatever I want, I take. I will take you, my Pete.'

He tried to smile again. It was a feeble attempt, and no more than a meaningless creasing of his features.

'Tania, you must not be foolish. You can't force me into this. No one can — not even you.'

Abruptly, she turned her back on him. In that position, she asked: 'The American legionnaire — he is your friend, is he not?'

'Certainly. He doesn't think very highly of me at the moment, but he is my friend.'

'And the *capitaine*?'

'He is my commanding officer. Such people do not usually strike up friendships with legionnaires.'

'But you like him? You respect him?'

'I do. We all do. We would not say so among ourselves, but we all know him to be a brave man and a good man.'

'So! And you would not like to see the

knives at work on them, would you? You would not sentence them to death — a very slow death? The knives cut portions out of them, my Pete. Out of their stomachs.' She faced him again, her face still a consummation of fury.

'That will happen to them — if you do not come to me. I swear it!'

The last remnants of colour had drained out of Pete's cheeks. But his voice was firm.

'I don't doubt you, Tania. And if I agree?'

'If you agree, the life of every legionnaire will be spared, and they will be helped to the coast — after we have dealt with the column.'

'El Zanal has already given us that guarantee, in exchange for co-operation.'

'It is not good to rely too much on my brother. But I, Tania, keep my word. *I* say they will be unharmed.'

Pete became aware that he was holding something. It was the wine goblet, still full. He drank it quickly.

He said: 'I have no choice, Tania.'

She was beautiful again. The fury had

faded and gone. She glided close to him and put her arms over the tops of his shoulders. She did not seem to notice that there was no answering movement from him. He remained still.

And she said: 'There is one other condition, my Pete. No one must know that you were foolish and I had to use threats. All must think that you have joined with me only because you want to. I have humiliated myself before you tonight. I will not have others know of it. And now, my Pete, you are free. You are with me and one of us. You do not go back to the legionnaires. You do not work with them. You are mine, and you please only me . . . '

13

The Last Hours

A Dylak stood at the foot of the steel flagpole. He fumbled for a while, his fingers clumsy and unfamiliar with the task. Then he started to pull at a long, slender rope.

The Tricolour of France went up over Fort Valeau.

It ascended slowly, uncertainly. And when it was at the top its blue, white, and red vertical stripes remained limp and folded, for there was no breeze that day to stir it.

But the spectacle satisfied El Zanal. He smiled as he watched from the compound. Then he turned to the group of heavily guarded legionnaires who stood near him.

'A convincing touch, I think,' he said. 'I appreciate that the column is not due until nightfall, and the Tricolour must come down at sunset. But even if the colonel's column does not see it, it is not a wasted effort. It gives a touch of veracity. It suggests that things are normal. And that, of course, is vital to my operation.'

There was a smooth assurance about El Zanal just then. It contrasted starkly with the haggard face of Monclaire.

Monclaire was not the type of man who swore much. But he uttered an oath which was horrible in its detail and lucidity. Then, mastering himself, he said: 'Can nothing convince you that this is madness, El Zanal?'

'Nothing — for it is not madness, *capitaine*. It is an expression of sanity. Violent sanity, yes. But that has been forced upon me by the French.'

'*Ah non!* You demand the right to dominate and terrorise other peoples than your own, and you are surprised that France does not listen to you! But whatever happens tonight, El Zanal, I know that in the end the Dylaks will suffer terribly.'

El Zanal rustled his robes.

'*Capitaine* . . . now that the day has arrived, you must not forget that we have come to terms. You are to assist me in exchange for your lives. Remember?'

Very, very faintly, Monclaire said he remembered.

Then he looked over the open compound.

The Dylak tents were coming down. Groups of warriors were carrying them into the buildings.

In the centre, the horses were being assembled into two sections. One section was being forced through the wide doors which led down into the magazine.

El Zanal followed Monclaire's eyes. He said: 'I am glad that the magazine is so commodious, *capitaine*. We'll be able to get several hundred of the animals in there now that we've cleared the munitions out. The others, we are driving out eastwards. Tomorrow we will recover them. They will naturally return here in their search for water.'

A Dylak approached with four Lebels. He put the rifles at El Zanal's feet.

'These,' El Zanal said, touching one of

them with his foot, 'are for the use of the sentries. They are unloaded, of course. I am going to put a Legion sentry on each rampart immediately.'

Monclaire shrugged.

'You are premature. It is only midday. The column cannot be here for at least eight hours.'

'That is so, *capitaine*. But, as I have said, I want to induce an immediate atmosphere of Legion routine. Then perhaps it will be easier for you all when the time comes for you to play your parts.'

He paused, then added: 'Now, *capitaine*, please select four of your men. Let them each take a rifle and put them on the ramparts. They can be relieved at your discretion. I will not interfere with your military practice.'

There was a shuffle among the legionnaires. Then a mumble in a Scandinavian tongue. And something small and brown sped through the air and splashed against the side of El Zanal's face.

It was the last tiny remnant of Corporal

Diepel's tobacco.

Diepel had moved in front of the others and was standing level with Monclaire. There was a desperate intensity about him. The intensity of a man who has had enough. Who can't take any more. It showed in every pockmark of his face.

It was not bravado. It was more than that. Not courage. It was something less than that. It was simply the unfettering of a man's character. Diepel was the world's typical corporal. When he could (which was for the first few hours after he drew his meagre pay), he drank too much. And as often as not, he got himself into a brawl. He had a taste for women. All sorts of women. Shape and size did not matter to him at all, and age very little.

He was a bit of a bully, a bit of a braggart. He could lie (but not very convincingly) if it suited his purpose. He could steal — but only if the article was of trivial value.

But there was one thing that Diepel could not do for long.

He could not disguise his feelings.

To him, that spit of tobacco was more

than a spontaneous expression of disgust. It was also a sacrifice. He had been conserving it for two days in a corner of his mouth, holding it secure within the hollow of a rotten tooth.

It was to be a short-term sacrifice. But perhaps Diepel, because he was like all the other Diepels, knew that.

El Zanal looked at him for a long time. Diepel looked back.

Very slowly, El Zanal extracted a square of silk from the sleeve of his robe. Punctiliously, he cleaned his face. He dropped the square on the ground.

He was still looking at Diepel but addressing Monclaire when he said: 'You should induce a greater sense of discipline among your non-commissioned officers, *capitaine*.'

Monclaire's haggard aspect became even more noticeable. He was torn between the duty of protecting Diepel and the natural instinct to express sympathy with him.

He said slowly: 'It will not happen again.'

'You are right, *capitaine*, it will not.'

El Zanal made a gesture to the guards. It was a detailed and vaguely obscene gesture.

Three of them grabbed Diepel and dragged him further apart from the others. Then two of them twisted his arms behind his back. The third drew out his double-edged stabbing knife.

It glittered silver before it sank into the depths of Diepel's stomach.

Diepel screamed. As the wounded in the sick bay had screamed. Like a woman.

When it was over, El Zanal said: 'I think you will now understand the necessity of your complete co-operation.'

Monclaire said to himself: 'When the column approaches I will shout a warning. Somehow I will get the words out before they knife me . . . '

Gina said to himself: 'I won't be afraid. I'll shout. Perhaps one word will be enough . . . '

And Rex said to himself: 'Maybe if I only scream like Diepel did, it'll do. It might let the column know something's wrong. Anyway, I've just gotta try something . . . '

But El Zanal might have been reading their thoughts. Before he left them, he said: 'I have selected the legionnaires who will be on duty when the column arrives. They are not the type who will give trouble. You, *capitaine*, are not one of them. Nor is the lieutenant. Or that American. You will all be kept well away from the rampart.'

★   ★   ★

Daylight was fading.

Only the livid tip of the sun was to be seen above the western horizon. The sky had aged into a weary grey and the dunes beneath it were dull like old copper.

A cool breeze had come, and it was flapping the Tricolour as a Dylak warrior brought it down from its mast.

Pete looked out of the officers' mess-room window. He had moved in there with Tania when the tents were taken down that afternoon. But the luxury of the tent was still with them. The deep carpets, the multitudinous cushions, the chairs, the quartz goblets, the wine. And Tania.

She came up to him and looked with him across the compound.

A sentry stood on the west ramparts. A Legion sentry. He paced from end to end. Then paused. Then paced again. It was exactly right. No one could possibly know that the Lebel slung over his left shoulder was unloaded. That the pouches round his black leather belt were empty, too. That even his bayonet had been snapped, so the hilt in the scabbard was all that was left of it.

And no one outside the fort could possibly know that soon, at the first sight of the approaching column, the sentry would be joined by Dylaks. But the Dylaks would be invisible to those outside. They would crouch behind the stonework, with knives pressed into the sentry's body.

Tania touched Pete's arm. He did not move.

She said: 'Another hour or two . . . that is all . . . and it will be all over. Perhaps you will feel better then. But don't look out there, my Pete. It makes you think too much. Turn to me. Look at me.'

He turned. She was gazing up at him. The heart-shaped locket was on her breast.

Without knowing why he did it, Pete touched the locket. A monogram was etched into the gold. *MdA.* The initials of Maria d'Anton. She did not resist while he fingered it. He found the catch. It sprang open. And within, a watercolour miniature was revealed. It was the face of a man wearing the uniform of the French army of nearly a hundred years ago.

A face like Tania's. The eyes were the same. The features, fine and arrogant, were the same. The hair, lush and black, was the same.

But the sum total did not tally. For there was no evil in that face. Only strength. The strength of Pierre d'Anton, marshal of France.

Pete looked from the portrait to her.

'You always wear it,' he said. 'Why?'

She looked away for a moment. Then she gazed direct at him again. But she did not answer.

'Tell me — why do you wear this? Are

you secretly proud of your French blood, Tania?'

She laughed. It was a strangely ugly sound. And it surprised Pete. It was like hearing flat, musical distortions emerging from a Bechstein.

He let the locket, still open, fall away on its short chain.

'Answer me!'

The laughing ceased. But there was still a harshness about her that was reflected in her voice.

'Proud of my French blood! How can you think that? You want to know why I wear this locket. I will tell you. I wear it as a penance. I wear it to remind myself always that within me is the blood of the people I hate, so I must be yet more ruthless, more terrible in my struggle against them . . . Now look, my Pete. I will show you what I think of my French blood . . . '

She held the tiny locket in front of her. She spat upon the watercolour portrait.

Pete saw her throat.

The same throat which had tempted him before. It was tempting him now.

And this time the feeling did not pass. It stayed with him. It possessed him.

He put out his hands and they circled the slimness.

The harshness had gone from Tania. She was smiling, a little surprised at what she took to be a lover's gesture. She tried to move closer to him, but his hands held her away.

It was only when his thumbs dug deep into her throat that she knew what he was doing.

She did not panic — for there was no cowardice in Tania. She did not resist, either. He saw only the pain of utter sorrow in her eyes. And the tears that had formed in them.

It was then that he knew that he could not do it. He could not kill her.

But she was only half-conscious as he carried her towards the cushions.

He tore away part of her robe, and with it he bound her wrists and legs. Then he forced open her mouth and pushed a piece of silk deep into it.

As he stood up, Pete saw that she had recovered. She was watching him. The sorrow had gone from her eyes. Now they were without real expression. Just flat, puzzled. Almost like those of a bewildered child.

Pete had not intended to speak to her. But he had to do so. He spoke as though in a dream.

'I had to do this, Tania,' he said. 'There was no other way. Goodbye . . . my beautiful, savage lady . . . '

She was still watching him as he moved out of the room.

★   ★   ★

The last of the daylight had gone. And the moon was not yet up. Outside the fort there was only the stirring of the night. The heavy flapping of the wings of a vulture making for its home among the rocks. The cold hissing of the breeze. The swirling of little eddies of sand. There was plenty for the ears to catch. Nothing for the eyes to see.

On the west ramparts, just over the gates, there stood the legionnaire without a name. They had never given him a name. Not the barrack rooms, in the camps, in the fort. True, at roll call he answered to some Balkan syllable. But no one took any notice of that. He was known — when he was known at all — as the Fool. Or *Sciocco*, or *Narr* . . . or any of the foreign equivalents. So long as they meant Fool.

For he was not like other men. He was apart from them, and seemed to like it that way. He did not talk with them, he did not drink or gamble with them. He seemed incapable of understanding anything but the simplest instruction.

The Fool spent long hours by himself looking fixedly at nothing.

Sometimes he fumbled in his tunic pocket and produced a faded and tattered photograph. It was of a massive and repulsive-looking middle-aged woman swathed in a Balkan national costume. It was rumoured that the Fool had murdered her — in which case it was probably the only sensible act of his life.

This was the man who had been selected to give the first challenge when the column arrived.

El Zanal had made a wise choice. The Fool would do as he was ordered. Even he knew the routine of challenge and recognition. And he would not be much concerned by the Dylak knives which were pressing against his lower body. He was too stupid for that.

He hitched his empty Lebel to his shoulder and stared blankly into the blackness.

Legionnaire Ducco had been dramatically promoted.

For a few brief moments he was to be the orderly officer. It was he who had been selected to confirm and check the identity of the column from the fort walls. It was he who would give the order for the gates to be opened.

Again, a wise choice.

For Ducco was one of the world's scavengers. And he had scavenged the world. He had whined for coins in gutters, he had bludgeoned money out of frail people in dark places. He had thieved, cajoled and bullied his squalid way from Valparaiso to Verona. Until he had felt compelled to retire into the Legion.

With, of course, the mental reservation that he would desert when it was safe to do so.

But Ducco's itinerant life had left him well-equipped in one direction. He had a mastery of many tongues. He could fit himself into many characters. Therefore he would have no difficulty in simulating the part of Lieutenant Gina.

In fact, as he stood outside the guardroom with the Dylaks round him. Ducco felt faintly pleased. Gina's uniform fitted him well. He liked the flattering hang of it. The expensive cut of it. It was only a pity that there was a dark tobacco-juice stain to spoil the breeches.

★　★　★

They smelled the horses before they were halfway down the steps to the magazine. The sickly odour of congested animals hit them like a blanket.

Monclaire said: '*Dieu!* Is this where you are putting us?'

El Zanal smiled as a guard opened the big doors. 'It is, *capitaine*. I need not concern myself with you while you are here. If you attempt any commotion — any movement, even — the beasts will kick you to pieces.'

It was true enough.

Like all magazines, the one at Fort Valeau had been made far larger than was strictly necessary to accommodate the munitions. Large areas of free airspace had been provided to prevent overheating and the possibility of spontaneous combustion.

Now all the munitions, all the arms, had been moved out. The long, wide underground space was packed with horses. The wretched animals were pressed so close to each other that each rested its head over the back of another. All were frothing at the mouth and showing the whites of their eyes.

Rex said: 'They need watering. They'll go crazy unless they drink!'

'They'll be all right for a few hours,' El Zanal told him. 'They will be freed immediately the column has been dealt with.'

The guards pushed them inside the

doors. Monclaire first, then Gina, then Rex. And after Rex, a dozen other legionnaires who were not wanted or could not be trusted.

The horses whinnied, and one or two of them kicked against the sudden increase of pressure. As the doors slammed and were locked, the legionnaires were each held between the animals' powerful, sweating bodies.

After a few moments, Rex said softly: 'If we so much as shout, you know what'll happen . . . ?'

Monclaire nodded.

'*Oui*. They'll take fright. And we'll be crushed to death. Or kicked.'

There was a sudden shuffle among the horses a few yards away. Hooves clattered on the stone floor. The pressure became more intense. Gina gave out a groan. He was held between the hindquarters of two white beasts.

Rex took a chance. He managed to twist round and slap one of them — but not hard. It moved slightly, and the pressure on Gina eased.

Rex said: 'There's only one thing to do.

We've got to turn ourselves into standstill cavalry. We've gotta get ourselves onto their backs — and somehow we're gonna have to stay there.'

Very slowly, very gently, they started to pull themselves astride the twitching backs of the nearest animals.

14

Arrival at Valeau

There was, of course, genius in the make-up of El Zanal. The power of leadership, too. The power which could inspire men to accept death. As the three warriors had accepted it when they destroyed themselves to create the gap.

And he also had another important asset. He was scrupulously careful. His every important action was the result of meticulous analysis, of judicial weighing of the known facts. Then, always, he checked and double-checked against the possibility of error.

In these, the final moments, he was doing just that. First, he visited the gates.

In the darkness, they were undetectable as hurriedly made substitutes. They looked heavy, massive, safe. And they were secured, as fort gates were always secured, by a huge beam.

He transferred his attention to the guardroom. Four legionnaires were standing at ease outside it. A fifth legionnaire, in the uniform of a lieutenant, was strutting up and down. El Zanal regarded him curiously and congratulated himself. Instinct had told him that Ducco was the man for the part. But he had not realised how completely right he had been. The fellow was indifferent to everything save the fact that he was in the uniform of an officer. He was almost believing that he *was* an officer. El Zanal smiled. Ducco might as well enjoy his brief time of self-importance. It would soon be over. Soon, everything would be over for him . . .

That stupid legionnaire was standing very still and looking out over the desert. He looked like the tiny pinnacle of a great monument. The Dylaks who crouched round him were invisible. But El Zanal knew they were there all right.

So far — excellent.

With a hand on his jewelled dagger, he moved quickly towards the compound buildings. Lights shone from the windows, making yellow splashes on the ground. There was an air of assurance about those lights. They suggested that all was well within — that this was still a fortress of France.

He did not enter immediately, but turned round the north wing of the buildings and came into the eastern side of the compound.

There, it was as though a huge mass of faintly moving shadow was pressed against the walls.

Occasionally, a light from the windows glinted on a bare and cruel blade. Or the blue, pencil-like barrel of a Piet showed up as a slender line.

Eight hundred warriors were assembled here. These were his main striking force. These were they who would charge round each side of the compound buildings and encircle the Legion column once the gates were closed behind them.

Eight hundred . . .

Yet such was their discipline, such was their silence, that it was almost impossible to believe that more than a tenth of that number was there.

He retraced his steps and entered the buildings.

Oil lamps were spluttering and flickering in the bare corridors — another touch of normality. In the long main corridor they reflected on the faces of his remaining two hundred warriors. These would stream out of the doorways, and with their Piets they would create the first confusion among the column.

El Zanal was satisfied.

All the dispositions were made. All orders were clearly understood. There was nothing to do now but retire to his room next to Tania's and wait.

And, as he walked towards it, he allowed himself the luxury of anticipation.

In his mind's eye he could see it all. The gates opening. The Legion column marching in while sentries at the guardroom presented arms. The column would draw up in a long file preparatory to being dismissed . . .

The gates would be closed and barred behind them.

That would be the moment. The supreme moment of massacre. He, El Zanal, would fire his silver-hilted pistol in the air. At the signal his warriors would charge . . . There could be no possibility of effective resistance. Most of the legionnaires would be dead before they had time to realise what was happening. The others would reel and stumble in the confusion, their minds bewildered, until they too were cut down. The chances were that he would not lose a single warrior.

El Zanal smiled gently.

He was sweeping down the quiet, unoccupied section of the buildings. His sandaled feet made a flopping echo. He listened to it, amused.

Then the smile faded.

He heard another sound which was new to his ears. The sound of breathing. It was close to him. It came from the shadows between two lamps.

El Zanal was about to make a sharp challenge. He did not have the opportunity. Something that was akin to a wild animal projected itself at him.

As he fell over backwards he looked into the contorted face of the English legionnaire.

★ ★ ★

Pete had no clear idea of what to do when he left Tania bound and gagged. He was aware only of a determination that something — anything — must be done.

It had not been an easy decision to reach, for so long as he did not interfere with the Dylaks, the lives of Rex, Monclaire, and the others were safe. He knew he could trust Tania's word on that. But, in the end, he realised something else. He realised that most of the legionnaires (all who mattered) would rather die in an attempt to stop the massacre, rather than sit back quietly preserving their own skins.

That had been the reason for his attack on Tania. Her ruthless sordidness had merely served to touch it off.

He had only taken a few paces away from Tania's room when he saw El Zanal approaching. Pete drew into the shadows.

A plan — a rough and fantastic plan — was taking shape in his racing brain.

Pete waited until El Zanal was less than a foot away. Then he threw himself at the Dylak. He did not punch him, he did not kick; he did not get a substantial grip on him. He simply crashed against him.

And as they went down, Pete was aware of one vital fact.

Silence!

He must work without noise.

Pete's right hand groped along El Zanal's robes. At the moment when they came into violent contact with the floor, he found the jewelled knife. It slid easily out of the scabbard. Before El Zanal fully knew what was happening, Pete had the blade at his throat.

He pressed it gently. It cut like a razor. A thin streak of blood followed the edge of the steel.

'Make any sound,' Pete said softly in El Zanal's ear, 'and I'll drag this across your neck.'

El Zanal's body became rigid. He was afraid. And he looked afraid.

Pete said: 'Where is Monclaire?'

At first El Zanal did not answer. Pete gave the blade a fraction more pressure. It opened a deep and lurid wound. Then El Zanal decided to speak. He spoke very faintly, as though he were choking: 'In the magazine . . . with the horses.'

With the horses!

Pete recalled hearing Tania say that some of the horses were to be hidden there so that they would be immediately available.

The horses . . .

A hollow thundering started in his brain. Like hooves. Then it died away. He heard another sound. And this was no figment of the mind. It was footsteps. He looked up. A Dylak guard was standing at the far end of the corridor, his puzzled eyes probing into the shadows where they lay.

In that second he forgot about El Zanal. Subconsciously, he moved the knife away from his throat. El Zanal took the opportunity.

He twisted his lithe body and threw Pete aside. Then his long fingers went for Pete's eyes — feeling, groping, to gouge.

Pete jerked his head aside and a reflex action — the result of long training in unarmed combat — prompted him to do the right thing.

He slammed his knee between the crutch of El Zanal's legs.

The result was paralysing. El Zanal's jaw went slack, his lips turned inwards, his whole frame became limp.

There was a flashing movement when Pete had the knife raised to drive into El Zanal's helpless breast. If the Dylak guard had hesitated for one additional second, he would have done so. But even as the blade was poised he heard footsteps rushing towards him.

Pete twisted to his feet and ran for the open compound.

★ ★ ★

He emerged on the west side and dropped panting to the ground so as to avoid the lights from the windows. There, pressed against the wall, he paused. He had to think. He had to know precisely what he was going to do.

El Zanal would be incapable of any sort of action for several minutes. That was certain. And it was probable that the guard had not recognised him in the shadows. Therefore, there was not much likelihood of an immediate hunt.

The next move was to reach the magazine. To reach them without being seen.

The only way was to crawl along the outside of the west compound wall. The other side was crammed with Dylaks. So were the middle corridors inside the building.

It was a faint flash of the old cynical, self-composed Pete which caused him to say as he started his crawl: 'This is no life for a gentleman. I think I'll retire from this army . . . '

It was the sheer concentration of the Dylaks that made it easier for him. That side of the fort had been deliberately planned to look normal. The only Dylaks there were hidden in the guardroom and kneeling on the ramparts. They were too far away to see one man easing towards the double doors which led down to the magazine.

It was a long crawl. Fully eighty yards. Pete's already damaged body was aching anew when it was completed.

There were no windows, and therefore no light near the doors. It was safe to stand up to examine them.

As he did so, he groaned involuntarily. Then two consecutive events caused his spirits first to rise in optimism, then to freeze in fear.

The first was when he saw that the big key had been left in the lock. That was natural enough. The Dylaks had no reason to believe that anyone would attempt to cause trouble from the outside.

The second was when he heard — very faintly — the distant crunching of many marching feet. And mingled with it were the familiar extra sounds of men on the march. The almost musical tinkling of equipment. The creaking of leather shoulder straps. The massed and heavy breathing. Sounds you could feel rather than hear. Sounds which would be inaudible in a few men, but were distinct when created by several hundred.

And he heard the Fool.

He heard his thin challenge from the ramparts.

'*Arreté!*'

And, more faintly, an answering command to halt from an officer of the column.

Pete pushed open the magazine doors. As he did so he wiped sweat from his face onto his sleeve and said: 'God! It's too late . . . too late . . . they're here!'

It was picking a nightmare out of a man's mind and saying to him: 'Live this. It's really going to happen!'

It was showing a man the ultimate inferno and telling him: 'You're walking into this. You don't want to, of course, but you won't be able to help yourself.'

It was not real, that wild rush down the shallow stone stairs. It did not seem real when he saw the Dylak at the bottom.

The Dylak was squatting on the floor. His Piet lay over his knee. He was looking up in mute astonishment at Pete. Then his hand grabbed for the automatic rifle.

There were ten of those steps between Pete and the Dylak. He gathered himself to jump — hoping that he would land on the Dylak before the Piet went into action. He pushed his arms behind him for balance. And as he did so, something scraped against his side. It was sharp. Something he had forgotten he was holding. It was El Zanal's knife.

Pete had never thrown a knife before, but he had seen it done once in a wine-shop brawl at Algiers. He changed his grip to the tip of the blade and flicked it spinning through the fetid air.

He scarcely realised that it had penetrated hilt-deep into the side of the warrior's throat. He did not notice that the Dylak was in his death throes before he threw himself down the last few steps.

Grunting, sobbing, Pete fingered the second door. It was almost a duplicate of the outer one. But this was locked and there was no key in it. He fumbled his hands over the Dylak's robes. No key there, either.

Pete picked up the Piet rifle and cocked the firing pin. He moved the control ratchet to the rapid-fire position. Then he bawled something through the door. He did not know what it was. He didn't care. There was an answering call from within. A call from several voices.

Then he heard Rex shout: 'Can you get the door open, bud? It's kind a tedious in here.'

That voice steadied him. It cleared his brain.

He called: 'I'm shooting the lock in.'

A two-second burst from the Piet was enough. The door drifted outwards on its creaking hinges, while cordite fumes caught in his dry throat.

Inside, he glimpsed a maze of animal confusion. He saw Rex clinging to the mane of a bucking horse. Monclaire doing the same. And all the others.

Pete felt that he wanted to vomit. And there was a strange feeling of compression in his head.

Through a thick mist he saw Rex jump clear of his horse and force his way out of the chaos. He felt Rex's arms round him.

Pete managed to say: 'The column's arrived . . . they're here . . . '

Then he fainted.

★   ★   ★

All save two of the legionnaires got out of the magazine. Those two slipped. They were pulverised by hooves. Nothing could be done for them. Anyway, there was no time to do anything. For a bestial madness had seized the horses. Many were charging out of the magazine and slithering towards the steps.

Monclaire, watching with the others from the shelter of the wall angle, saw the possibility.

He picked up the Piet from where Pete had dropped it. Then, twisting round as far as he dared, he sent a stream of lead over the animals.

And the panic became still worse. Scores of the horses kicked each other to death. Many more were maimed. But a few — less than fifty of them — managed to get up the shallow steps. And into the compound.

The trap was opening slowly. But it was also opening well.

Legionnaire Ducco had especially distinguished himself. At exactly the right moment he had mounted the ramparts. In exactly the correct tones of cultured respect he had conversed with the staff major. And, as a touch of pure embellishment, he had said, 'Dinner is waiting for you in the mess room — Monclaire is there!'

Yes, the strutting, thieving, mendacious Ducco was having a memorable day.

And when the gates creaked open, he stood to attention with the rest of the legionnaires outside the stone guardroom. He forgot about the Dylaks who were concealed just behind him in the deep shadows, forgot about their knives. For Ducco was the orderly officer. He wallowed in his brief moments of sham glory.

Ducco composed himself for the command which would bring the Lebels to the 'present' position.

But he did not utter it. It would have been useless if he had. For his words would have been ignored against the competition of a sudden thud of hooves and a burst of shouting from the east side of the compound.

The disturbance came as the first ranks of the column, led by Colonel Panton, were marching in.

★   ★   ★

Frightened animals, from the smallest to the large, cling to cover when on the run. They avoid the open ground. Thus the first of the crazed beasts to get in the compound turned round the outside of the building, galloping close to the wall. And the rest, on the same basic instinct, followed.

They charged into eight hundred Dylak warriors.

One mad horse can create terror among a large number of people. The more people the greater the terror. The effect of nearly fifty beasts was concentrated carnage.

The Dylaks reacted in two separate ways. Most of them believed in a fuddled manner that they were being attacked by cavalry. They opened fire with their Piets. The others, realising that the horses were their own, tried to capture and calm them. They could not have known the pure impossibility of the task. They were trampled on and crushed.

In a few seconds the panic had spread from the beasts to the men. And the men could not be blamed for this. Shooting, fleeing, cursing, they scattered like seed.

★ ★ ★

And the Dylaks inside the compound . . .

They heard the firing from the east side. From the wrong side. They heard the hooves. They concluded that the other warriors were meeting a shock assault — which was true enough.

After a brief hesitation, they changed their plans. They emerged out of the east doors to give help.

And they added to the ghastly chaos.

Half the column was inside the fort

when Colonel Panton decided to halt. He gave a hand signal. Then he turned to his staff major. He made a gesture towards the cacophony.

'What's — what's happening? *Dieu!* Is the garrison drunk?'

Then he saw the first of the robed figures. They were running, and their robes were silhouetted against the lights from the west windows. The colonel's facial muscles became limp. His eyes glazed.

The staff major said: 'We can't remain like this, *mon colonel.*'

Panton did not answer.

The staff major added, much more tersely: 'Something is wrong. Very wrong. We cannot remain halted with half the column inside the fort and the other half outside it.'

Panton was wrestling a mental paralysis. And a sudden physical weakness. The sight of the Arabs had turned his brain into a turgid, impotent slime. And had transformed his never very powerful body into a quivering mass of useless flesh.

'*Mon colonel!* The situation calls for

immediate action . . . '

Panton achieved a feeble nod. A reluctant nod. Like a man giving the signal to a firing squad at his own execution.

'*Ah, oui*. I — I will leave this matter entirely in your hands, Major.'

The major smiled. It was a grim smile. He turned his horse and shouted: '*Avant!*'

The column continued into the compound, the rhythmic crunching of their boots blending with the sounds of distant chaos. They were still marching when the major gave a second order.

'*Fusil!*'

The legionnaires unslung their Lebels. Safety catches were pressed forward.

Ducco had been watching hard. And Ducco had been listening hard. Yet he could not fathom what had happened. But one fact was obvious to his crafty mind. Something had gone seriously awry with the Dylak plans.

And that was a serious matter for Legionnaire (Acting Orderly Officer) Ducco.

He gave the problem rapid consideration. It resolved itself into the simple question of asking which course of action would be likely to produce the least harmful results to his own skin.

He would gladly continue his loyalty to the Dylaks — if the Dylaks were going to be victorious.

But what if it did not turn out that way? In such a case, Ducco considered it essential that a valiant Ducco be found fighting for and under the Tricolour. And he could easily explain his apparent willingness to pose as the orderly officer. He would point out that he had done so only in order to give warning to the column.

Ducco listened to the Piet guns and saw the flashes.

He was shrewd enough to know that the Dylaks could only be firing upon themselves. And the thud of hooves had been easy enough to identify, so somehow the horses must have got free and caused confusion.

It was that realisation which decided Ducco — almost.

He would, he knew, gain gratitude and possibly honour, if he were to warn the major of what was happening. But there was the matter of the Dylaks who were crouching just behind him and the other legionnaires. Ducco recalled their words. They had said that the merest intake of breath to utter a warning would result in the plunge of a knife. His shifty eyes switched from side to side as he sought a safe way out.

The major was less than ten yards away. He was sitting on his horse and watching the column move in. It ought to be possible, Ducco thought, to make a sudden jump and get to the other side of the major's horse before the Arabs could strike. Then, under the major's protection, he could give his message.

Ducco jumped forward. It was as though he had been ejected by a powerful metal spring. He reached the horse in three strides. Grasping its bridle, he swung himself round it. The staff major looked down on him in astonishment. The astonishment increased when Ducco almost screamed at him: '*Mon officier* . . . it's the Dylaks . . . they have the fort . . . they . . . '

A Dylak knife made a gentle, almost graceful arc through the air. It emerged out of the shadows. It reached its apex at the central point between delivery and target. It descended over the saddle horn of the major's horse. It finished very slightly to the left of Ducco's chest. He had met an easier end than he deserved. The blade itself entered and stopped his mean little heart.

If the staff major retained any capacity for further astonishment, he managed to conceal the fact. He glanced at the fallen Ducco. And then in the direction from whence the knife had come. He gave a brief order. A section of twelve legionnaires detached themselves from the marching column. Another order, and they raised their Lebels and fired into the shadows. A splutter of Piet fire was returned, but the aim was bad. Only one legionnaire was hit, and his was no more than a slight shoulder wound. The Dylaks were rattled. After a second volley from the Lebels — this time aimed at the Piet flashes — the local resistance ended. There was silence, save for the shooting and the cries of panic around the compound buildings.

The orders that followed were brief, but their effect was efficient and dramatic. Within minutes the whole Legion column was within the compound and had formed into a double file along the entire length of the fort.

'Legionnaires — *baionettes!*'

Nearly four hundred hands streaked towards four hundred scabbards. There was a series of quiet clicks as the twenty-inch lengths of steel were locked under the barrels of the Lebels.

'*Avant!*'

In open order and with bayonets fixed, the legionnaires advanced upon the compound buildings.

As they got close, a company on each flank detached itself and moved round to the back. And presently the heavy, almost ponderous explosions of the Lebels were mixing with the comparatively light-sounding and chattering fire of the Piets.

⋆　⋆　⋆

El Zanal . . .

He became conscious within a few minutes of receiving the blow from Pete. But it was many minutes before he was capable of being assisted to his feet.

Then, leaning heavily on the shoulder of a guard, he was told that the column had arrived.

El Zanal managed to smile faintly.

'Do they suspect?' he asked.

'No,' a pasha told him. 'It is as you planned.'

El Zanal tried to forget the pain in his groin. He tried to concentrate on an immediate course of action. And he decided not to interfere with the operations against the column. He was, he realised, in no condition to help, and he might well be an encumbrance. He would emerge when the column was massacred to congratulate his warriors. Until then he must rest.

He decided to go to Tania's room.

It was likely, he knew, that the English infidel would be there. But in that case the Englishman would be told to go. And while the column was being exterminated, he, El Zanal, would try to reason Tania out of her stupid infatuation.

It was madness for her to associate in this way with a legionnaire, and El Zanal had no intention of tolerating it for long. But he had agreed to it for the time being because other and more critical events were pending. He had not wanted to be disturbed. It had been easier to give way — temporarily.

But the time had now arrived to exert pressure on Tania. It would not be easy, he knew. It may take a few days. But it had to be done. The notion of his sister and a legionnaire . . .

As he was helped to her room, El Zanal mentally flinched at the thought.

At first, when he entered, he thought that she was merely absent temporarily. He indicated a chair and told a guard to help him to it. It was only then that he saw Tania. His eyes first caught a flicker of movement in a corner. When he realised what and who it was, he took in a slow, heavy breath. His face was limp with anxiety as he watched a warrior unfasten her bonds. When she was free, El Zanal ignored his own pain and knelt beside her.

'Who did this?' he whispered, although he knew the answer. There could be only one answer.

There was a strange flatness about Tania. A total lack of reaction which was new to her. And there was no tone or expression in her voice as she said: 'He did it.'

El Zanal twisted his lips.

'I, too, have met him. It seems . . . '

He did not finish the sentence. He stopped because another sound had become apparent. The sound of hooves. They were circling the buildings. He looked questioningly at his guards. They looked equally blank, equally confused.

But not for long.

They understood when a Dylak rushed in. Such was his excitement that his salaam was little more than perfunctory. Then he said: 'The horses — they're free . . . '

El Zanal hobbled to the window. There he saw the horses emerging from the magazine. And he heard the shouts from the warriors on the east side. He heard, too, the first of the Piet shots.

He peered towards the main gates. Nothing could be seen there for the moment.

Then something emerged out of the dark. An odd, formless shape which was moving with almost absurd precision.

It was the Legion column!

But in the second that he recognised it, he also heard more Piet fire. This came from the direction of the guardroom. And mixed with it was Lebel fire.

El Zanal turned away from the window and gazed desperately round the room. Deducting from the basis that the horses were free, he was able to reach a fairly accurate assessment of what had happened. And he was confronted by a devastating fact — he had lost the advantage of surprise.

There was only one possible course open. He must get out into the compound and somehow restore order and sanity among his warriors. That done, it might still be possible to overwhelm the column. But speed was the first necessity. Speed . . .

He grabbed a Piet from one of the guards. Then he hobbled out. Tania followed.

★　★　★

Pete . . .

He felt as though he were drowning. As though someone was dragging him by the feet through rough water.

He was surprised to find there was no water near him, and that he was propped up against a corner near the magazine entrance.

Rex was standing over him. And Rex was saying: 'It's okay, bud. The column's cleaned this place up.'

Pete struggled to his feet. His knees felt weak. He staggered towards the steps. Rex put a hand on his shoulder.

'Take it easy. There ain't no sense in going up there. You can't help any. You can only get in the way, and you might walk into a slug.'

Pete shook his head wearily.

He said one word: 'Tania.'

Rex tightened his grip on Pete's shoulder.

'Don't worry about her.'

'I've got to go to her. I left her bound and helpless. Anything may happen to her . . .'

Rex moved his face close to Pete's. He looked hard into Pete's eyes.

'That woman ain't no good to you, bud. Forget her.'

Pete smiled at him. It was the smile of a man who knows, but cannot explain. Then, slowly and precisely, he removed Rex's hand from his shoulder.

Rex stood very still as he watched Pete climb the stairs and turn towards the compound.

★　★　★

Colonel Panton . . .

The colonel had emerged from a temporary and discreet retirement.

During the first surge of events, he had eased his horse over to a quiet place near the main gates. Confused though he was, the colonel saw that if things went wrong his most urgent requirement would be a swift and convenient line of retreat.

For long minutes he sweated in the saddle. He listened anxiously to the bang of Lebels, the rattle of Piets, the hammering of hooves, the cries of frightened and agonised men. He screwed up his eyes and tried to see what was happening, but without much success.

Then an important fact occurred to him. It was that the Piet fire had almost ceased. But the fire from the Lebels remained disciplined and continuous.

Very cautiously, Colonel Panton rode towards the compound buildings.

As he got nearer he saw that there was now little action on this, the west side. The bodies of several Dylaks lay about, some of them twitching and moaning. And a few legionnaires were on guard at the doors. But the main activity was to the east.

And there could be no doubt as to what was happening. There was clearly no need for he, the colonel, to take undue and irresponsible risks by a personal investigation. He would wait here.

As he waited, the colonel felt a glorious glow tingle through his limbs, and then reach up into his mind. The last of his fears vanished. The situation became remarkably clear to him. And full of astounding possibilities.

He had arrived to find that the fool of a captain had allowed the fort to fall into the hands of the Dylaks. And the Dylaks had been waiting in ambush . . .

But what had happened . . . ?

He, Colonel Panton, had retrieved the desperate situation. His forces had engaged and routed the Dylaks. In a single stroke he had recaptured the fort and ended the Dylak menace.

Did ever a punitive force produce such startlingly satisfactory results?

Non, never!

True, he had deputed some of his authority to his staff major. But that had been merely a matter of detail. He obviously could not attend personally to every fragment of the action. The solid fact remained that the responsibility had been his. After all, if there had been

250

failure to report, he as colonel would have been blamed. Therefore it was only just, was it not, that he should accept the credit for success?

But Colonel Panton decided to show generosity to his staff major. He would not — as he had threatened while on the march — make an adverse report about him.

The colonel turned his horse and retreated again into the utter gloom. He did not wish to be observed. For the call of drama was upon him. He wished to enact a moving scene . . .

He saluted an imaginary general. His head was slightly bowed in becoming modesty. There was a catch of half-controlled emotion in his voice.

He said into the darkness: 'It was time for swift action, *mon general*. The situation — it was incredible! I did what I feel you, *mon general*, would have done had you been there. I am glad that I was so successful . . . '

He smiled at the general. And the general smiled back. Other senior officers crowded round to congratulate him.

Sitting in the saddle and concealed by the night, Colonel Panton extended his hand and moved it up and down, as though shaking other hands . . .

★　★　★

Pete emerged from the magazine and into the compound. The cordite-tainted but comparatively clean air helped to clear his head. The feeling of nausea faded. Keeping close to the wall, he skirted towards the east side.

He passed a Legion sentry who was guarding one of the doors. The man looked at Pete curiously, and for a moment it seemed he was going to challenge him. But after hesitating, he let him pass.

Pete reached the window of the room where he had left Tania. He stretched up and looked inside. He saw the remnants of her silk bonds on the floor. But that was all. No one was in there.

He whispered to himself: 'God . . . where is she . . . ?'

But as he asked the question he knew

the answer. The fanatical, and utterly lovely Tania could only be in one place. She could only be where the last Dylaks were still resisting.

Pete broke into a run as he turned the corner of the compound buildings. Then he stopped suddenly. The moon was rising. Its light was still thin, but it was enough. Enough to see into the depths of hell.

The horses had gone. Their first panic over, they were now clustered somewhere by the north wall, shaking and exhausted. But they had left behind them hundreds of mangled Dylaks. Few had been killed outright by the hooves. Most still lived, their splintered bones cutting and torturing their flesh. They crawled aimlessly, moaning and praying for death. Others, but not so many, had been finished by slugs from the Lebels. They lay still. They were fortunate.

But a few of the Dylaks were still fighting. They had been forced back against the angle of the east wall of the compound. From there they aimed an occasional wild burst of fire at the long line of legionnaires which was closing in on them.

As he absorbed the situation, Pete realised that the Dylaks were placed between him and the legionnaires. From where he was standing he ran an imminent risk of being hit by a Lebel.

He was about to move away when he saw her.

He saw Tania.

She was standing in the centre of the desperate group. The top of her robe was torn and through it her pale skin shone dully. Her raven hair was wild and it splayed down upon her bare shoulders. She was holding a Piet. And she stood erect, as a symbol of feline defiance.

Her brother was at her side. El Zanal also held a Piet. His oaths were like the spit of a cat.

Pete drew in a breath. He was going to call her. Going to tell her she must surrender. But he did not. The words faded before they were formed. For she saw him.

And as they looked at each other, it was as though all of time, all of life, had become nothing. The stars ceased to move in their heavens. Men ceased to love and hate and struggle upon their little earth. It seemed as if everything was still, as Tania looked at him and he looked at Tania.

It was El Zanal who broke the weird magic of the moment. El Zanal saw him. His lips came back in a humourless, deathly grimace. Then he raised his Piet and aimed it at Pete. Pete did not move. He could not move.

Tania screamed. It was not a scream of panic or pain. It was one of feminine fury. And it was directed at her brother. In the moment before El Zanal squeezed the trigger, Tania threw herself in front of the barrel.

Her slim body quivered and jerked as though being subjected to a series of high-voltage shocks. Then, like a fragment of paper, it fell softly to the ground. El Zanal scarcely had time to know what he had done. Even as he looked down, stupefied, at her body, a Lebel bullet made a hot and neat hole through the middle of his forehead.

Pete walked to her. He stooped and picked her up. He brushed that wild hair back from her face. There was no fury, no evil in her countenance now. It was calm. As it had never been calm before.

He walked with her into the shadows.

Rex saw him and was about to go to him. But Monclaire said: 'Leave him, *mon ami*. He is best left alone.'

And Pete knew it was best, too, as he held her to him.

For in this moment only the stars and the sky seemed to understand.

We do hope that you have enjoyed reading this large print book.

Did you know that all of our titles are available for purchase?

We publish a wide range of high quality large print books including:
Romances, Mysteries, Classics
General Fiction
Non Fiction and Westerns

Special interest titles available in large print are:
The Little Oxford Dictionary
Music Book, Song Book
Hymn Book, Service Book

Also available from us courtesy of Oxford University Press:
Young Readers' Dictionary
(large print edition)
Young Readers' Thesaurus
(large print edition)

For further information or a free brochure, please contact us at:
Ulverscroft Large Print Books Ltd.,
The Green, Bradgate Road, Anstey,
Leicester, LE7 7FU, England.
Tel: (00 44) **0116 236 4325**
Fax: (00 44) **0116 234 0205**

SHERLOCK HOLMES: THE FOUR-HANDED GAME

Paul D. Gilbert

Holmes and Watson find themselves bombarded with an avalanche of dramatic cases! Holmes enrols Inspectors Lestrade and Bradstreet to help him play a dangerous four-handed game against an organization whose power and influence seems to know no bounds. As dissimilar as the cases seem to be — robbery, assault, and gruesome murder — Holmes suspects that each one has been meticulously designed to lure him towards a conclusion that even he could not have anticipated. However, when his brother Mycroft goes missing, he realises that he is running out of time . . .